WINTER GAMES

by Kyell Gold

WINTER GAMES

Published by FurPlanet
Dallas, Texas
http://www.furplanet.com

ISBN 978-1-61450-088-9
Printed in the United States of America
First trade paperback edition: September 2012
Cover and all interior art by Sabretoothed Ermine
"Hurry Up" title font by Larabie Fonts, *http://www.larabiefonts.com*

For Sierra
with love

CONTENTS

2012: ARRIVAL

Sierra Snowpaw checked in to the Lonnegan Ski Resort on February 28th, 2012, with all his worldly possessions in a large hiker's backpack and small computer bag. He did not have a job, nor a plan, and as of midnight the following night, the room in one of the elegant, fiery red lodge buildings would be the closest thing he had to a home.

"Business or pleasure?" the pine marten at the desk asked as he took Sierra's credit card.

The snow leopard looked down. "Sure," he said. It probably didn't matter that he wasn't going to be able to afford this stay, because without an address, it would take the credit card company a good couple months to track him down. Given a good couple months, Sierra could straighten out—well, *nearly* anything.

"There's a corporate retreat here," the pine marten said. "Sonoma Systems. Are you with them?"

The marten's name tag read "Bret," and he had a nice, slender face with kind eyes that looked up at Sierra, whiskers twitching. "Oh. No. Just here alone." Sierra smiled down. "Pleasure, I guess."

"Excellent." Bret tapped some keys on his terminal. "You'll be over in the Elm Lodge. Let me just get your room keys. Do you need equipment rentals?"

"Yeah." Sierra leaned forward, resting his elbows on the counter. Bret had no rings on his fingers, a silver ear stud in both ears. He wore the uniform of the resort, but his scent was individual: his natural musk enhanced with…Sierra breathed in. Bobbi Jean's 'Temptation for Males,' that was it. It had a nice sweet aroma that was popular with gay guys, who also liked that they could call it "BJ Temptation." It had been a while since he'd gone looking for a short-term hookup, but of course that was just another kind of story to tell someone. The question was more, did he want to try?

Well, why not? He certainly wasn't going to have anything else to do tonight, and if the past fifteen years were any indication, he wouldn't have anything to do the other three or four nights, either. He'd followed stronger clues to deader ends.

He sized up Bret: young, single, probably very open to flirting from hotel guests, especially if they were well-off and cute. Sierra knew he could fake the former and act the latter. "I just decided to come down

here at the last minute. Do you have any recommendations for some
trouble I could get into?"

Bret hesitated, and then a smile curved up his lips, though he didn't
look at Sierra. "Let me get you a ten percent off coupon at the rental store
on the property. How well do you ski?"

"Used to quite well." Sierra lifted his eyes to the rustic logs framing
the desk, the pictures of athletic arctic wolves and hares in dramatic
skiing poses against the white snow and green pines of Mount Gondorf.
"Haven't been in about five years. Five? Yeah."

"Where's the last place you went?" The printer on his desk spit out
three coupons. Bret collected them efficiently and folded them into a
stack.

"Chartrier-sur-Neige," Sierra said. The stories were always easiest
when they were mostly true.

Bret whistled. "Fancy. Well, our slopes here are as good as any over
there, if not better. Just cause there aren't many people here don't mean
it isn't top-rate." He grinned. "I can't promise the same about the food
unless you stick to the resort restaurant. It's just there across the lobby."
He pointed behind Sierra. "Um, what else. You just missed the big music
festival over in White Springs. 'Alternative' music." He wrinkled his nose
and then leaned forward, taking a chance. "I hate calling them that. You
know?"

Sierra smiled back. "Defining them in terms of what they're not,
not what they are." He knew the argument, also knew that defining a
genre as "alternative" appealed to people who wanted to be something
different. That was the story they were telling. And Bret, because he liked
alternative music but not the name, wanted to be different—but not too
different.

"Exactly!" Bret's smile widened.

"Remember Valhalla?" Sierra said, and the pine marten nodded. "I
got to meet them once."

"Wow. I liked them. Too bad about Joey Stone. Did you talk to him?"

Sierra's tail twitched as he nodded. "Just, like, 'hello.' But it was
exciting," he said.

"I bet." Bret dropped the coupons on the counter and tapped the
small pile. "These are coupons for the rental at the ski area. Ten percent
off skis and boots, ten percent off any purchase you make there, that's
good for all four days of your stay, and then this one gets you a free lift
ticket when you buy two days."

Sierra put his large paw over the coupons. "Thanks." He looked down at the pine marten, who let his paw linger next to Sierra's for just a moment longer than needed.

"Not a problem, sir. And here's your room key." Next to the coupons, he slid a plastic card with a photo of a skier against a bright blue sky, and a folded map. "I found a room in the Aspen Lodge. It's a newer lodge, and this room has a nice balcony that looks out onto the mountain."

"Thank you. That sounds really lovely." Sierra slid his paw over to cover the room key as well. It held a small amount of warmth from Bret's paw. The pine marten was still looking at him attentively, waiting for the hook he knew Sierra was going to drop his way.

Sierra paused and then said, "You've been really helpful. Is there some way I could repay you?"

1997: ARRIVAL

The mountain behind the school rose higher than anything Sierra had seen in his life. Thin lines carried rows of bars, some with people on them, about two thirds of the way up to the jagged tip of the mountain, a claw at the end of a finger jabbed into the sky. Sierra extended his own claw, holding his finger up to the mountain, and then followed a chattering group of arctic foxes through the glass doors marked "Tartok Ecole Internationale."

The hardwood corridors bore the marks of hundreds of claws, but Sierra kept his retracted, his feet silent amid the tik-tik-tik of other footsteps. While the other students filtered into their homerooms, Sierra had to ask directions to the principal's office and then wait for the secretary there to tell him where to go. As a result, announcements were already echoing over the school's PA system by the time he opened the door to room 20.

In his hurry to get into the room, he stumbled, and then the door closed on his tail. Nobody in the class laughed outright, but they snickered behind their paws, the arctic foxes and ermines and ring-tailed lemurs and tapirs. On the far side of the classroom, a female snow leopard sat up straight, eyes wide.

"You must be Sierra." The red fox in the tan blazer at the front of the room smiled. He gestured to the back of the room. "I'm Mr. Dvorczak. You're coming to us from the States, right? Where in the States?"

Sierra nodded, waiting at the front. "Howard High in Millenport." Before Mr. Dvorczak could ask the next question, he said, "My dad's in the military."

"So you've moved around a lot. Any foreign languages?"

Sierra shook his head. "No, sir." Well, not unless you counted Unix, he said to himself.

"We'll be speaking English in most of your classes." He glanced down at his desk. "There's an open seat in the back row next to Mr. Coyote, if you don't mind—"

Mister Coyote? He had barely glanced up to see that 'Mister Coyote' was, in fact, a coyote, when—

"Sir! Mr. Dvorczak!" The female snow leopard had her paw up in the air and was half out of her seat. "Paula is going to move to the back." She beamed at the sulky hedgehog next to her, who stood at that remark with an armful of books and stomped to the back row. "So Sierra can sit here." She rolled her Rs in her throat in a very French sort of way.

"Natasha, I…" Mr. Dvorczak sighed and made notes on his paper. "All right. Fine." To Sierra, standing awkwardly in front of the rows of small wooden desks, he said, "Go ahead and sit next to Natasha."

Sierra made his way through the desks to the third row, where Natasha stared at him with a fixed, hungry smile. He tripped on his way, this time over an outstretched foot that had been pulled back when he looked down for it. The wolf to whom it belonged stared straight ahead, snickering, his tail tip flicking.

The snow leopard hurried to his desk and slid into it. He curled his tail around the base and folded his arms in as tightly as he could, wedging his long legs under the desk. It was hard to imagine how his first appearance in his new classroom could have gone much worse without his pants actually falling down in front of everyone.

"I'm Natasha," Natasha hissed to him over the last few announcements. Sierra had been trying to listen to them, which was difficult with the tripping and seat-changing, and also because he'd missed the first few, and also because they were in French.

"Sierra," he said back under his breath, aware of Mr. Dvorczak's large black ears at the front of the room.

"Are you taking French, Italian, or German? I'm taking German because I already speak French. I came here from Lutèce, but I lived in Crystal City until I was ten."

"Mmm," Sierra said. "I'm taking French."

"Oh. Well, it's okay. We'll have other classes together." Her ears perked. "And I can help you with your French! Maybe you can help me with math. Are you any good at math?"

Sierra nodded. "I'm okay," he said.

"I can't believe there's another snow leopard here. Paula was hoping you were a hedgehog. Can you imagine that?"

The bell rang and everyone grabbed their books and got up. He turned around to look at the hedgehog as he stood.

In the back row, still seated, a rangy coyote was leaning back in his chair, paws behind his head. His arms and legs looked even thinner than Sierra's, and below his large tan ears, his amber-brown eyes were staring right at Sierra. Paula the hedgehog had already gathered her books; she walked along the windows not looking at Sierra or Natasha

at all.

Sierra found himself wondering whether the coyote would be as tall as he was if they stood side by side. The careless ease with which he occupied the chair and then stood, collecting his books under one arm, reminded Sierra of Rey. Except for the tail, of course; the coyote's bushy brown tail swished slowly, where Rey's had coiled and flicked, when he hadn't had it looped over one arm.

Natasha tugged at his sleeve. "Don't pay any attention to that coyote," she said in a low voice. "Everyone who hangs out with him gets in trouble. And don't ever get the milk here if you're used to milk from the States. It's terrible."

"Okay." Sierra tore his eyes away and walked with Natasha to the front of the room, and out to math class. Maybe having a friend who spoke French wouldn't be all that bad. Besides which, if he sent his parents pictures of the two of them together, it would go a long way. And she was pretty cute, too. "What do you guys do for fun around here after school?"

"You're not eighteen yet, are you?"

"Last month."

"Oh!" She brightened. "Then you can get us drinks."

"I can't get you drinks," Sierra said. "It's illegal." He controlled the little flutter in his stomach.

Natasha snorted. "There's no drinking age here. Mostly the bartenders don't check, but there are a lot of tourists from the States so sometimes they do. You don't have a girlfriend yet, do you?"

"Er." Sierra told the truth, if not the whole truth. And perhaps it was the whole truth; Rey hadn't written him in ages. Not that he would know where to find Sierra now. And if Natasha was offering to be his girlfriend…images flashed through his head: holding her paw, a picture at a dance, introducing her to his parents. "No."

Her smile stretched even wider, and she looked ahead to where two of the arctic foxes were walking holding paws. "There's a big dance at the Embassy and the students here usually get invited. It's quite the affair. But that's in the spring. Until then…some of us like to go up to the lodge. We could even go down by the lake."

"Does anyone ski?"

"Some of the kids have year passes, and they run up as soon as school gets out at three." She wrinkled her nose. "It's like an obsession with them. Do you ski?"

He shook his head slowly. "No."

"Good. Oh!" She spotted the Valhalla sticker on his notebook. "Valhalla's coming to play here in the spring. My God, I can't wait. Do you like them?"

"Oh, yeah. I have all their albums." Over his parents' protests, though if they'd listened to the lyrics of his favorite song, "Carousel," they might have understood better why he listened to it over and over. And they might not have let him. "Do you have tickets?"

She grimaced. "They go on sale in two months. I hope Daddy gets me tickets. The music is pretty terrible, and this place is boring."

"It could be worse. Believe me." He said it just the way his parents had said it to him.

She either didn't hear him or didn't care to ask further, which was fine with him. "But we'll be able to go to the dance together. Oh, this is going to be a wonderful year!"

Something brushed Sierra's leg. The coyote walked quickly past him, tail swinging back and forth. Sierra's whiskers twitched, and he caught the faintest whiff of the coyote's musky scent, with a light spicy fragrance atop it. "So what's his deal?" he asked Natasha.

She grimaced. "He's a loser. Just ignore him, and if he offers you anything, just say no."

Sierra nodded, but even as Natasha kept talking, his eyes followed the black-tipped bushy tail down the hallway.

2012: VOICES

Bret slid paws down Sierra's rear. He said, "Mmm. Been waiting to do that all night. You've got a great ass."

"You too," Sierra said, mirroring the movement and squeezing the pine marten's nice, rounded rear in return.

"You like your tail stroked or no?"

"Uh. Yeah." And no sooner had he said it than Bret's little paws were sliding down, the marten pressing closer against him to get farther down the tail. Sierra caught a moan in his throat.

It had been a while. Kiran had left three weeks ago, and sure, Sierra had jerked off in that time, but he'd been busy selling his furniture and closing out his job and so there'd been no time to go look up one of his friends-with-benefits ("one of" being somewhat generous, as the list was currently down to one, who lived in another city). The feel of another body pressed to his pumped heat to his hard shaft; the smell of arousal waiting for him to release it sharpened his desire; the excitement of meeting someone new quickened his breath, set his heart to racing.

Fingers fumbled; belts came undone. Shirt buttons popped hastily open and fabric fell to the ground. On Sierra's king-sized bed, they confirmed each other's experience with the easy removal of each other's boxers and the casual acceptance of nakedness. They grinned and explored the areas of fur previously hidden, to a soundtrack of 'mmms' and 'aahs,' of anticipatory, quickening breaths.

When Bret's paw had settled on Sierra's sheath, the pine marten said, "I'm usually on top."

"Me too." It was an easier answer that saying he didn't feel like having the pine marten inside him, that he just wanted to hold someone and feel that someone's body shudder with release, and to feel his own release, and share the warmth afterwards.

"There's always mouths."

"Mouths are fine," Sierra said, and it wasn't sixty seconds later that the pine marten had pushed him back on the bed, coaxed his shaft out of its sheath, and dropped his muzzle down onto it. His tongue flicked along it as his lips drew up and down, and Sierra closed his eyes.

It took him a little while to come, as it usually did his first time with a new person. But it also had that tinge of excitement, that first time he was opening himself up to someone, the jerks and spasms of his body, the gruff pants that turned into a teeth-clenched moan, the tightening of his legs around Bret's chest as the pine marten gulped and sucked, his lips tight around Sierra's trembling shaft. And with the release of sexual energy came the release of sexual tension, and a moment of nervousness: now he was just in a room with a horny stranger.

He relaxed; the moment passed, and it was okay. Bret wasn't a complete stranger; they were united, at least for tonight, with a single purpose. The pine marten licked his lips and looked at Sierra with an expectant gleam in his eye, and Sierra propped the back of his head up with pillows and said, "C'mon up here and kneel."

Bret scrambled eagerly up the snow leopard's chest, and Sierra wrapped a paw around his thick erection, glistening with pre around the tip. Holding the base delicately between two fingers, Sierra lapped up the underside of the shaft, getting a sharp taste of musk. Bret arched his back and made a happy squeaky noise, and when Sierra licked up again, Bret made the noise again. Sierra twitched his tail, grinning, and did his best to hear that adorable noise again.

He planted his paws on the marten's rear, and opened his muzzle to take the thick shaft all the way in. Bret's hips went willingly back and forth, his shaft hot and slick through Sierra's lips.

He did have a nice cock, and a nice body, so Sierra didn't really mind that it took him a while to work up from a slow, lazy thrusting to more excited and jerky movements. He leaked a lot, but the taste wasn't objectionable, and Sierra's jaw wasn't close to being tired yet. He closed his lips around the skin, explored the surface with his tongue, and perked his ears to the increasingly high-pitched sounds.

It all culminated in a long series of rapid-fire squeaks and thrusts, Bret's paws on Sierra's head as his body tensed and shuddered, and then a loud cry from the pine marten. "Uhh…yeah…yeah…yeah!" His hips shoved all the way forward, his cock thrust against Sierra's tongue, and the snow leopard felt and tasted the hot splash of musky seed.

He held the marten's rear and closed his eyes, feeling the warm shudders of the other atop him subside, moans sliding down into breathy pants. Bret's tail flicked back and forth over Sierra's sheath, and then the marten's whole body sagged. He slid out of Sierra's muzzle, slid down his chest, and wrapped his arms around the snow leopard's neck. "Mmm. Nice," he said.

Sierra hugged him back, eyes still closed. Bret's head rested on his shoulder, his breath warm on Sierra's neck. That was nice, too. Even the last month or so they were together, Kiran hadn't been very snuggly. They'd shared a bed, because neither of them wanted to take the symbolic step of sleeping alone on the futon, and anyway, the futon had been one of the first things sold.

But long after Bret's breathing had dropped into an even rhythm, Sierra remained awake. They'd shared a rich meal at the lodge restaurant (on Sierra's tab), but the food wasn't keeping him up. His tail twitched restlessly, and finally the room felt stuffy enough that he rose, put on pants, and quietly went outside into the cool air.

It had been a nice night. Bret had been the perfect dinner companion: happy to talk about movies and books, popular music or video games, as uninterested as Sierra was in anything personal that had happened prior to that night. They'd made pleasant, famliar small talk throughout the dinner, confirming only that they were both unattached and still eager to get back to Sierra's room for the real purpose of the date.

Bret had hurried Sierra back along the path, complaining of the cold air on his thin fur though they both knew the real reason for his haste. Now the snow leopard enjoyed the cold air on his bare chest as he walked out of the Aspen Lodge and onto one of the flat river-stone paths between it and another building. The stars winked overhead in the spaces between the clouds, and on the mountainside, the lights of snowcats darted to and fro, as if some stars had fallen and were tumbling down the mountain.

Run! They'll get us!

His muzzle wrinkled into a half-smile at the memory, and then a grimace. He resisted the urge to dash away.

Shadows stirred, movement on one of the balconies in the opposite building, second floor. A large shadow, lots of weight. Bear or tiger, maybe a wolf, carrying a spare tire. A second person was there, too, much lighter on his or her—her, he guessed—feet.

"Come back inside," a gruff voice, said, the bear-tiger-wolf.

Sierra, still basking in his post-coital glow, grinned at the pre-coital pair. He couldn't catch their scents, not in the dry air out here with the breeze blowing up the mountain, but the tone in the deep voice said volumes.

Then it said, "Too exposed out here."

Sierra frowned—that didn't sound pre-coital—as a light voice laughed in reply. "Oh, who's going to see us?"

And that voice wasn't female. No, it wasn't female, and he *knew* that voice, knew the confident, cocky swagger to it.

"Get in," the bear-tiger-wolf said. The balcony creaked with footsteps, then the glass door slid closed.

Sierra couldn't move, could hardly breathe. He'd been thinking of the voice because of the snowcats, from that time. That was all it was. He'd thought he'd recognized that voice in the past and been wrong.

But even as those thoughts crossed his mind, he was striding, then running for the door, the bright-lit arch of stone in the dark wall. He yanked it open and ran inside, up the stairs, and then stopped in the hallway. The balcony had been—opposite this room? Or this one? He stared at the rooms, and then put his ear to each door, looking up and down the hall first to make sure he was alone.

No sound came from either. Had he been mistaken? Or were the two being quiet?

He ran outside again, made out the balcony in the darkness, and then hurried back inside the building, where he met two ladies descending the stairs. Their eyes widened when they saw him, and only then did he remember that he was running around without a shirt. He gave them what he hoped was a reassuring smile.

On the second floor, he still couldn't tell for sure which room matched up to which balcony. He kept looking up and down the hall in case someone else came back, and the more he thought about it, the more he was convinced he'd been mistaken. It had been the memory and the light male voice, that was all.

So he padded back to his room. Bret didn't wake as Sierra came in and took off his pants, and slid in next to him. Bret fit nicely into his arms, even rolling into the embrace. He curled one paw over the pine marten's shoulder and breathed, lifting the lighter marten and lowering him again. He closed his eyes.

Who's going to see us?

He was imagining things. He had to be.

1997: PICTURES

"Who's going to see us?" Natasha teased her fingers through the fur under Sierra's chin.

"Mr. Dupont, that's who. He gave Marianne and Gino detentions just for holding paws."

Natasha brought her lips closer to Sierra's. "He's in the math class we're supposed to be going to."

Her breath smelled of her chlorophyll gum. "So what if he comes looking for us?" Sierra looked to his right, at the dark, empty classroom, and then to his left, at the wide-open hallway.

"He won't do that for at least another minute. Sixty seconds. This'll take ten." And with that, she just pressed her lips to his. A moment later, her body followed.

Her breasts rubbed against his chest, pushing his sweater-vest around as Natasha wiggled her body up and down. Her tail curled around, attempting to twine with his. He didn't actively resist it.

"Hey." A voice snapped them apart, though Natasha's tail took its time unwinding from his. They both turned to see the rangy coyote, sleek silk blazer dwarfing his skinny frame, looking at them with a grin and big perked ears. A silver hoop dangled from the base of the right ear.

"Oh, it's you," Natasha said.

"Just wanted to tell you to get to math class before too long. Don't want to miss Dupont's lesson plan today." He talked to Sierra as if they were old friends, though this was more words than they'd exchanged in the two weeks Sierra'd been going to the school. The coyote's voice was light and soft, with a hint of a cultured British accent to it.

"We can make it up." Natasha scowled. "You've ruined our first real kiss."

"Shame," the coyote said. "But trust me. This is worth it."

"What," Sierra asked, leading Natasha out of the dark alcove and then releasing her paw as soon as they were in the hallway, "is he going to explain something in English for once?"

The coyote, walking ahead of them, half-turned his head. His earring caught the light. "Oh, you'll see," he said, his black-tipped tail swishing as he walked. Sierra watched the tail and the shadowy curves of the tight pants below it, mostly hidden by the long drape of the blazer, then averted his eyes in case Natasha noticed him.

He didn't know what it meant that he liked looking at the coyote. It wasn't a gay thing, because he didn't really imagine having sex with him. But there was something about the slender body, and the confidence with which he carried himself, that made Sierra just want to *be* with him. Even though most of the class ignored him, Sierra'd never seen the coyote stumble or trip, or flatten his ears in embarrassment. "Hey," he said, impulsively. "What's your name?"

The coyote half-turned again and parted his muzzle just enough to show a line of sharp white teeth, the tip of a pink tongue curling around the canine fang. "Carmel," he said, as they arrived at the door of the math class, and gestured with a paw. "After you."

Natasha gave Sierra a look of annoyance, as if he shouldn't even be talking to the coyote, and marched into the classroom first. Sierra followed.

Mr. Dupont, a portly goat, tapped his desk with a wooden pointer, a nasty smile on his muzzle. "Well, Miss Demetriova, Mister Snowpaw, that will be one tardy each." He licked his lips as though each tardy was a delicious treat. "And Mister Coyote—"

"We had to stop at the principal's office," Carmel said smoothly, producing a paper from his pocket and dropping it on the desk. "Sorry for the delay."

The goat stared down at the paper as though Carmel had placed a live snake on his desk that was currently devouring those delicious tardy slips he had been so looking forward to handing out. Sierra expected Mr. Dupont to read the slip and ask why only the coyote's name was on it, because surely Carmel hadn't had the time to write all three names down—they'd have seen him. But the goat just swept the slip into his desk drawer and said, "Today we will be returning to quadratic equations. Please attend to the screen."

He tapped at the computer on his desk and the screen behind him lit up with a Powerpoint logo. Sierra took out his pen and notebook and scribbled down the date, taking a moment to review the previous day's lesson.

"The quadratic equation," Mr. Dupont droned, assuming his usual lecture voice, "describes a curve which intersects the x-axis at two points." The first slide appeared, a graph with a U-shaped curve in red. "With an equation for which the solutions are minus two and plus four, the curve will intersect the x-axis at these two points." Over the graph slid an equation with x's and powers and parentheses. Sierra copied them down.

He'd figure out what they meant later.

"You can always find the solutions for a quadratic equation with a simple formula." Sierra, still copying down the graph, looked up when he heard the gasps and titters from the class. Splashed across the screen was a buxom female gazelle cupping her breasts in both hands, her legs spread to show her shaved sex. She smiled invitingly out at the class.

"*Allez Monsieur Dupont!*" called one arctic fox, while Natasha, beside Sierra, gasped and hid her eyes.

"*C'est pas possible.*" The goat smacked the keyboard, and another slide came up, this one with a female mule deer bent over with her tail lifted, turned suggestively so her chest was visible in profile, small tusk highlighting a warm smile.

"Woo!" "*Formidable!*" The boys in the class were getting into the show.

"Sierra!" hissed Natasha.

"What?" He couldn't take his eyes from the screen. A stocky female horse was next up, on her knees with one hand between her legs and a pout on her long face.

"*Bellissimo!*" called Gino, and that started a discussion among the boys about which of the three was most attractive.

"Don't look at it!" Natasha hissed at him.

"Why not?"

"Quiet!" roared Mr. Dupont. He yanked a cable out of his computer, and the screen behind him went dark.

"Aww," chorused some of the boys.

Gino pointed. "Hey, you can still see the reflection in the window."

Indeed, the primary monitor showed clearly enough for them to see the next picture, a camel lady in a maid's outfit. "*C'est une chamelle!*" one of the ring-tailed lemurs at the front of the class said.

"*Widerlich!*" called an ermine.

"Be quiet! *Taisez-vous! Sied still!*" Mr. Dupont shouted. He turned the computer off. "Not a one of you must—" He stood and stared at the class, panting heavily, and then lifted his arm to point a shaking finger around the room. "One of you is responsible for this and I am going to find out which one."

"But sir," Carmel's light drawl came from two rows behind Sierra, "it was your computer. How could any of us have done that?"

The goat stared at the back of the room, and his arm came to rest with his finger pointed at the coyote. Half of the class turned to look. "Do not think, Mister Coyote, that you are not at the top of my list."

"Don't look at me," Carmel said. "I don't find camels very sexy, myself."

The class giggled, until Mr. Dupont slammed his fist down on his desk. "Detention!" he shouted.

"Really?" Carmel said. "I mean, that's your right, of course, but do you really want to explain to the principal that you gave me detention because I questioned your taste in jack-off material?"

The goat's eyes narrowed. "You little *espèce de…*" He gathered himself. "You will all spend the rest of the period completing exercises one through ten of chapter four, as well as *all* the bonus exercises. These are due tomorrow at the beginning of the period."

The class groaned, but Sierra heard Gino say to the fox beside him, "Fifteen math problems for a little peep show?" and the fox grinned back and made an "okay" sign with his paw.

"How could you just look at those things?" Natasha asked in a soft hiss as they started working on the exercises.

Sierra frowned. "They were on the screen," he said. "What was I supposed to do?"

"*Not* look." She heaved a long, exaggerated sigh. "You are a boy, I guess, and that's what boys do."

He nodded, a bit bemused. He wasn't sure why she would be mad in the first place, nor why he didn't particularly care that she wasn't. But he lowered his head and worked on his exercises, only once turning to look back at Carmel.

The coyote was lazily scratching at his paper with a pencil, in what looked like random movements, but he glanced up right as Sierra looked, as though he'd been waiting for that moment. When their eyes met, the coyote's earring caught the sun as his ears perked forward, and his lips curved slowly back into a smile.

2012: SKIING

Bret was already dressed by the time Sierra pulled himself fully into wakefulness. "Hey, sleepy," the marten chirped. "I need to go to my shift. You need anything?"

Sierra yawned and shook his head. "I'll go grab an energy bar or something."

"I left you a couple coupons for free breakfasts." Bret waved toward the desk. "By your laptop. Oh, hey, you don't have to pay for the wireless, by the way. I can give you a code."

"Oh. Um, sure." Sierra had already hacked into the wireless network and connected for free, but he never turned down a legit way to get what he'd already taken.

"Thanks for a fun night. If you're bored again before you leave, you know where to find me."

"Sure." Sierra smiled and raised a paw. "Yeah, it was fun."

He sank back onto the bed as Bret left, staring at the ceiling. He was going to have to do something about that cocky voice, coming out of the cold air and the past, or else he'd go crazy with wondering. His tail twitched against the bed, and he kneaded his claws into and out of the sheets. Occam's Razor said that it was just someone else with a similar voice. Sierra'd thought he'd heard the coyote's voice before, many times, and he'd always been wrong.

But it had been a calm, still night.

His stomach growled, reminding him of Bret's coupons. Better get some food in him. Then he could go find the room that let out onto that balcony.

He pushed himself off the bed and, after showering, went to his computer, to bring up the Tartok Alumni Newsletter again, the issue from January. There it was, the bit about the Lonnegan Resort, with the addendum, "Perfect place to take a leap." He bit his lip. "Take a leap" could mean so many things, but he'd thought of Leap Day immediately. So he'd come here expecting nothing, and then last night he'd heard the voice. And today was Leap Day.

Bret had drawn the curtains, and through the window, the mountain rose blinding white. Sierra walked to the window to look, touching fingers to the cold glass as he followed the progress of skiers down the white slopes cut into the green pine forests. Was one of them the coyote he'd been looking for all these years? They were little more than colorful

pixels sliding down a white screen from this distance.

He had to consider the possibility that he was just talking himself into this. There were to be no more doubts, no more hopes. He'd told himself that. This was going to be the start of a new stage in his life, and so he was going to investigate this and then he was going to go take a skiing lesson and be done with it.

So he went to the breakfast buffet and ate an english muffin and sausage with a big glass of orange juice while he spread out the hotel map. Annoyingly, the buildings were all different, so he couldn't just look around his own to figure out which room let onto the balcony. But he had an idea of where he had to go by the time he got up and left the coupon on the table.

The front door of the Birch building wasn't keyed, so Sierra strolled right in and made his way to the second floor. The simple corridor layout left little doubt which of the rooms let onto the balcony he'd seen the previous night. It had to be room 213—the one that was currently open and being cleaned by a cougar maid.

Sierra held his breath. He poked his head into the room and sniffed, but he couldn't catch any scent of the occupants over the cleaning and Neutra-Scent products. What's more, there were no bags on the floor, and—he craned his neck to see the reflected bathroom in the door's mirror—no toiletry products around the sink.

"Hello, sir." The maid waved at him. "So sorry, the room is not ready yet."

"Oh, I'm not here." Sierra put on his at-ease smile. "I was just looking for a friend of mine. I thought he was staying in this room."

"No, this room is empty. Checked out."

"I said good night to him here last night, though." Sierra waited patiently, but the maid just shrugged and shook her head.

He retreated into the hallway, tail lashing behind him. If Carmel had been here, had seen him or noticed that he'd arrived, and then left early… well, it'd be just like the coyote, wouldn't it? He stalked down the stairs and slammed the front door of Birch, kicking snowdrifts on his way back to the main lobby, where he dropped into one of the armchairs, folded his arms, and waited for Bret to be free at the front desk.

The pine marten broke into a big smile as Sierra came up. "Hi, sir," he said. "What more can I do for you?"

"I just want to know if a friend of mine checked out." Sierra lowered his voice to a whisper, leaning across the desk. "He's in 213 Birch, I think."

Bret's smile faltered. "I'm not supposed to do that," he hissed. "What 'friend'?"

"I didn't know he was here. I saw him on the balcony on the way back from dinner." The pine marten frowned. Sierra pressed on. "I would've called up and said hi, but you know, I was a little busy looking forward to something else. And now I don't think there's anyone in the room."

Bret glanced at the other desk clerk, a caribou who was currently occupied with a large bison whose fur practically dripped with jewelry. The pine marten looked back at Sierra. "Honestly," Sierra said with his best earnest demeanor, "I just want to find a friend of mine."

"All right." Bret tapped his terminal. "But you can't tell anyone."

"Course not." Sierra reflected briefly that it was nice to be actually intending to keep that promise.

"Okay. Yeah, looks like they checked out this morning. Seven a.m." He frowned. "They were supposed to stay two more days."

"With the Sonoma Systems conference."

"Yeah, there's like nobody else here. Weird. Wonder what happened. Anyway, so, yeah. Sorry."

Sierra nodded. He leaned forward a little more, making the movement look natural. At this angle he could barely see the screen, but he didn't dare look directly down. "You said 'they.'"

Bret checked the screen again. "Married couple." He met Sierra's eyes. "Didn't know he was married?"

"They were just dating last time I saw him," Sierra lied smoothly. Bret wasn't going to be distracted enough that he could lean over and look at the screen, so he leaned back from the counter. "Okay, thanks. I really appreciate it."

He half-turned, but stopped when Bret hissed softly at him. The pine marten looked over to his right again—the caribou was now pointing out the bison's room to her on a map—and then leaned across the counter. He whispered, "What was your friend's name?"

Sierra let the smile come over his muzzle again, and lowered his ears as if embarrassed. "You know, I mostly chatted with him online as Tor88, and he went by Tor when we met. I only used his real name once or twice, and I don't really remember it."

Bret glanced down. "Stevenson? Lars Stevenson?"

"Sounds familiar," Sierra said. "It could be him." Bret was pretty guileless, but there was always the chance he was testing Sierra, making up a false name to get the snow leopard to reveal his intentions.

"Well." Bret nodded. "That's the guy's name. Lars and Marie Stevenson?" He squinted at Sierra again.

"Yeah, Marie was the girl he was dating. I'll have to get online and ask him why he left early. Thanks a lot."

"Oh, it was nothing. Sorry—I have other customers."

Sierra nodded. There was a short line behind him. "I'll see you 'round."

Clouds swirled in the sky that afternoon, and a brisk breeze blew down the mountain. Sierra joined a small group of four people and an ermine with a yellow instructor's jacket outside the rental shop for skiing orientation. There'd been ten sign-up spots in the class, so it was clearly a slow time for the resort.

While the ermine went through the usual issues of safety on the slopes and how to attach the gear, the snow leopard watched the skiers on the slopes. It was easy to tell the lifers from the tourists, and the experienced tourists from the first-timers. Sierra honestly didn't know where he'd fit now. At one time, he'd been able to take black slopes easily, but that had been ten years ago. Five years ago, on his last skiing trip, he'd gotten a third of the way down a black slope—though they weren't called "black" over there; they had a system of stars—and wiped out spectacularly.

Sierra, it turned out, was the only one who'd skied extensively and been away for a while. There was one more moderately experienced skier. "I probably won't need to do much for you two," the ermine said. "You already know what to do, you just have to get used to skiing again. I'm going to be taking everyone on a tour, takes about half an hour, and we'll end at the Starlight lift. If you take that up, it's a really nice blue slope coming down."

"Thanks," Sierra said. He took one more look at the slopes and then followed the group on their way to the first green slope. Standing on the brink of the slope, he felt the familiar tightness in his stomach staring down the white curves. Even here on the green slope, where it would take him barely ten seconds to get to the bottom, his stomach fluttered.

But the flutter lasted only for a moment. Sierra pushed himself off and then he was sliding down the slope, wind in his fur, accelerating. The rush of wind and the hiss of snow under his skis filled his ears; trees and snow and other skiers flashed into and out of his sight. The curves of the slope rose up to meet him and he shifted his weight instinctively to accommodate them. Toward the bottom, he overthought a turn, and his skis clacked into each other. Stop thinking, he reminded himself. Just do it.

After three green slopes, he felt a little more confident. The ermine took them on the small slope that led back to the rental shop, then across the mountain and up to the restaurant, and then to the green slope at the far side, which ended very close to the resort itself. They ended the tour back at the restaurant, where Sierra and the sheep got onto the lift to go up the blue slope while the ermine took the rest of the group back down the green again.

"Nice to get back on the slopes?" the sheep asked as they shuffled through the line.

"Yeah." Sierra inched forward with his poles. "It feels really good. How long's it been for you?"

"Just a year." She looked up the mountain while Sierra looked back at the restaurant. "I was on these slopes all the time a few years back. Then I moved out east."

Two people got up from a table, taking their trash to the bright blue garbage can. One was a large skunk. The other was a coyote.

"Our turn," the sheep said.

Sierra started to turn to get onto the lift, and just as he did, he caught the flash of something metallic reflecting from the coyote's ear. "Wait!" he said, but the seat bumped his legs and tail, and he sat down automatically.

"What?" the sheep said as they lifted off from the ground.

"Thought I saw someone…" He turned his head again. It took him a moment to spot the coyote, walking away with the skunk, deep in discussion as they retrieved their skis. The coyote's skis were black and unremarkable, but the skunk grabbed a set of bright lime green skis. Those were the last things Sierra saw before his chair went past a large tree, cutting off the view.

1997: PUBLIC LODGE

"I start skiing lessons next week," Sierra said. "Have you ever tried it?"

"Do I look like I've had broken legs?" Natasha examined her claws one by one. "Trust me. It's much nicer down here at the lodge. There's a fire and chairs, the bartender speaks English, and everyone comes through here at the end of the day."

"So?"

"So they'll see us," she purred, taking his paw in hers.

Sierra let her. There certainly was a fire, and it kept the room warm to the point of stuffiness, not only from the temperature, but from the trapped scents of all the people sitting at the bar, in the plush chairs or on one of the long sofas, as they were. He had insisted on sitting next to the window, because Natasha refused to sit by the door, and the windows were the second-coolest places in the lodge. He had no idea how she bore it, with the same fur he had, but the heat seemed to bother her less.

Another perk of sitting near the window was the view. The lodge sat at the bottom of the mountain, but a hill sloped gently away down the side he was looking at, covered with pine trees. Through gaps in the trees he could see individual roofs, like brown Monopoly houses dropped in the snowy forest. "What are those?"

Natasha craned her neck to follow his gaze, her eyes half-lidded against the glare off the snow. "I'm sure I don't know. Maybe the people who groom the trails live there." She shifted her gaze to the bar. "Vincent just came on shift. Do you want a drink?"

He shook his head. "I'm okay."

She squeezed his paw and smiled at him. "It's so nice to be here, just us snow leopards, right?" As she got up out of the chair, she leaned over and tried to kiss him on the lips, but he shifted his head slightly and she got him on the nose.

From his chair, he could see just about everyone in the lounge. The dark faux-natural logs made it hard to distinguish some of the dark-furred species, and the scents swirled around each other confusingly: a beaver couple was impossible to see except for the wife's glittering earrings, and the husband's yellowed front teeth, which showed every time he laughed. Two male chamois laughed boisterously over in one corner, near a badger and a stoat.

The wide glass doors opened, letting in sun and breeze. A trio of arctic foxes tumbled in, laughing and shoving each other: Gino and Marianne and Carlo. Even across the lounge, Sierra could hear them arguing about who'd navigated the last slope the fastest.

"I was clearly in front," Gino said.

"In front of everyone but me," Carlo laughed, and the two began a high-speed Italian argument, which Marianne stopped.

"You were both just staring at my tail all the way down," she said in her accented English, and flicked that tail.

By this time, they were standing close to Sierra, the cold mountain air preceding them even as it warmed to the room. While Gino said, "*C'est beau comme queue, 'y a pas de faute de m'en occuper,*" Marianne greeted Sierra with a smile.

"Natasha here?"

He indicated the bar. "Getting drinks. Vincent is serving."

"Oooh, *bonne idée!*" She turned to Gino. "Come on, you can buy me a drink for letting a girl beat you."

"I will buy you a drink because you have a beautiful tail," Gino said, and off they all three went to the bar, the two boys raising paws to Sierra.

He grinned and watched them go. All in all, he would rather hang out with them than Natasha, but though they were nice enough, they were still species-cliquish. You could be with them, but not of them, not unless you were an arctic fox.

At the bar, Natasha and Marianne immediately launched into a squealing discussion of something or another that had happened or was going to happen at the school. Sierra turned his head and looked down again, past the white-iced pine trees to the small brown cottages, each one isolated.

"You've got to have money to have one of those," a voice said softly by his ear.

He breathed in coyote scent. Carmel must have slid in behind the foxes, while they were occupying Sierra's attention. "What are they?" he said, without turning.

"Private lodges. Ski-in, ski-out. See the trail leading down here to the lift?" A long brown-furred finger extended from the olive-green sleeve of the coyote's jacket, and Sierra did indeed see the faint ski trail it was pointing to. "I got to stay in one of them once. Veeeeery posh. Satellite TV and Internet, all the stations from home as well as the crap they show here. Hot tubs, too."

Sierra laughed. "We just watch movies."

"You and your folks?"

"Well…" he paused. "Just me, really. Dad's stationed…somewhere." He waved a paw. "I'm not supposed to say. Mom's there with him too."

"So you're on your own?"

"I'm staying with a host family. They're Deutsche wolves my dad met in the service."

"Sounds grim. Sauerkraut every night?"

Sierra laughed. "Every other. And veal and sausage and spaetzle. And that's about it."

The coyote crouched down, his voice lowering even further. The silver earring flashed as he turned toward Sierra. "You're missing out. There's so many good places here. Some night you should let me show you a good time."

"I don't get many free nights. I have to be home by 18:30. Then I do homework and—what?"

The coyote's mouth hung open in a laugh. "Eighteen-thirty? Oh, military. Anyway, there's ways around that. Your room has a window, right?"

"Sierra!"

He snapped his head around at Natasha's voice. She was striding toward him, drink in her paw, the arctic foxes trailing behind. "I asked you if you wanted something to eat."

But she was glaring behind him, and it was clear that her annoyance was only partially from his distraction. "I told you I'm okay," he said. He felt the movement of air on his whiskers with a brief flash of coyote scent, and he knew Carmel had gone.

"You said you didn't want anything to *drink*." She plopped down beside him. "Marianne and the boys want to get a pizza, only if you're going to have some we should get two mediums instead of one large, and if you don't want some then do you want something else, because I might get what you're having instead of the pizza if you're having something else."

"Pizza's fine," he said. "Anything on it you want."

"Do one with just cheese," Natasha said. "And the other one with ham and egg or whatever you want on it."

"I like the pizza with egg," Marianne said. "But no ham. See if they will do a white pizza…"

They went on arguing about the pizza. Sierra stole one look across the lounge at Carmel's olive-green jacket and tall brown ears, and the coyote flashed a look back at him, showing off his canines in a narrow smile.

"Sierra," Natasha said, indicating the three arctic foxes and the two of them. "The Polars are all going to see Titanic again and a dance tomorrow night. Can you come? To the dance, I mean, not Titanic."

"Sure," he said absently. "Sure."

"There's this nightclub Marianne's brother told her about. They play all the best new music from the States, but it's so hard to get in. And tomorrow night is the only chance I'll get because my parents are going down to Sarino for the weekend so I don't even have to be back by midnight." She leaned up against him and purred. "So if we get bored of the club, we can go somewhere else."

"I still have to be home by midnight," Sierra said, inhaling her scent, which was feminine and chemical with the Jean-Laurent-something perfume she liked to use. Her warmth against him wasn't bad, to be honest, and it was nice to feel like he belonged in the group of Polars, as long as he didn't think about the places Natasha was hoping she could go alone with him later. She was still technically underage for another two weeks.

"Your parents are so strict."

"My host family," he reminded her.

"Of course." She turned to Marianne. "Sierra's going to come along tomorrow."

The arctic fox smiled warmly at Sierra. "*Formidable!*" Her tail wagged, too.

Sierra relaxed, a smile creeping over his own muzzle. Natasha snuggled up against his side, and Gino put an arm around Marianne. Carlo just sprawled out in his large armchair with the clear drink in his paw; he bumped the slice of lime in it with his nose as he drank. Sierra met his eyes, and the green-eyed arctic fox raised his glass.

"Not drinking?" Carlo said.

"Not on a school night," Sierra said.

Natasha sniffed and sipped her own drink. "You won't drink tomorrow night, either."

"Ah," Carlo said, "If he don't want to drink, he don't have to."

"He wants to," Natasha said. "He's just such a good boy." She looked up at Sierra and purred. "Aren't you?"

"I have to be," he said.

"He's even so good he wants to talk to that coyote." Natasha took another dainty sip of her drink.

The arctic foxes all looked away or made faces. "Okay," Sierra said, "what's his deal? I know you said he gets people in trouble, but…I mean, who cares about Mister Dupont?"

Carlo laughed. "*Il camello!* That was brilliant."

"The thing is, it's not always just teachers he does things to." Natasha exchanged looks with Marianne. "His parents are diplomats or something and he thinks he's so clever."

"His father works for the American embassy," Gino said. "Mama knows him. She said he has his job because his wife's father is important in the government somewhere."

"His mother came to school once," Natasha said. "She wore some hideous rainbow outfit and had streaks of weird colors in her fur."

"He poured green dye on my tail." Marianne stuck her tongue out. "He said it was for the feast of St. Patrick. Something ridiculous."

"It was ridiculous," Natasha said. "St. Patrick's Day is in March."

"Oh, this was March," Gino said.

Marianne shook her head. "It absolutely was not. It was May, because it was right before the Diplomatic Academy Dance at the Embassy." Her ears flattened and her brow lowered. "I had to soak my tail in lye all night, and it was impossible to make it fluffy again. I hid it below my dress the whole night."

Gino caressed Marianne's paw. "You looked beautiful still."

"The DA ball is so stuffy anyway." Carlo waved a paw.

"Of course you could say that," Natasha said. "You've gone four times. I've never been." The glance she gave Sierra looked hungry for more than just pizza.

Marianne ran a paw through her tail. "That was my first."

She looked like she might cry, so Sierra changed the subject. "Did anyone do the math homework?"

Natasha reminded Sierra again the following afternoon to come by her place before going to the club. He waved good-bye, and before he'd even crossed the street, he spotted Carmel leaning up against the window of a jewelry store. The coyote tapped his earring with a finger, a slight smile on that long muzzle, and though he wasn't looking at Sierra, the snow leopard knew somehow that Carmel was aware of him. He hesitated, then angled his steps to bring him up next to Carmel.

"Looking for another earring?"

The coyote turned to look at the displays in the window and flicked his ear so that the silver earring rang against the glass. "Maybe." He looked sideways at Sierra. "You shopping for anything?"

Sierra shook his head. "I just wanted to ask you something."

Carmel's smile stretched wider with evident interest. The snow leopard took a breath. "Why have you been talking to me?"

The coyote raised his eyebrows. "Should I not?"

"No, I mean…" Sierra flattened his ears, feeling very warm though the air was chilly. "Everyone says you like to mess with people. So if you're trying to mess with me…"

Carmel's smile remained wide. "Don't?"

"Yeah."

"All right. Do your friends also think there might be another reason I'm talking to you?"

"They don't…uh, they haven't really…" Sierra thought about Natasha and her scorn for the coyote.

"They don't know, or they don't care?"

"A little of both, I guess." Sierra looked away, at the gold chains and rings arrayed in the window. The smell of snow was thick in the air, and together with the pine and lake smell that was always blowing through the city, he felt a little more at home.

Carmel's eyes met Sierra's in the reflected glass, in the light of the overhead clouds. "What do you think?"

2012: TRAILS

It wasn't hard to find the skunk who'd had the green skis at the Sonoma Systems mixer that evening in the lounge. His badge read Forrest Worther, which made Sierra instantly dislike him even before the skunk opened his mouth. "Well, hi there," Forrest said, edging closer to Sierra, his bulk and scent drowning out most of the rest of the room for a moment. "What can I do for you?"

Sierra stuck out a paw. "I'm here trying to get a job with Sonoma," he said, "and I thought that marketing would be a great place to start."

"Oh, son, we're not doing recruiting here. Unless you've got a particular sales pitch to make."

The way he was looking at Sierra was pretty familiar. Sierra flicked his ears and tried not to make his complete lack of interest apparent. "A friend of mine recommended me to you. A coyote?"

"Any particular coyote?"

"He's here at the lodge—I was just having dinner with him last night. Name's Car—um." Sierra scratched his cheek.

"Carson?" The skunk's eyes narrowed.

"Right. Carson."

"And he sent you to me to ask about a job?"

Sierra raised his eyebrows, playing off the skunk's suspicions. "Well," he said. "A job, yes. In a manner of speaking."

The skunk frowned. "He didn't mention anyone else to me. I just saw him this afternoon."

"Oh, well, I did ask him to let me approach you first," Sierra said. He was starting to get an inkling of what kind of "business" the coyote had been doing with the skunk, and that fit the profile of Carmel.

That didn't help matters. "He said the deal was just between the two of us."

"You know," Sierra said, "maybe I should go talk to him again. You know where he might be?"

"No, sorry." The skunk scanned the crowd and raised a paw. "Oh, Tamara! Just a moment. Sorry," he said to Sierra, "I need to talk to Tamara."

There was nobody looking at the skunk, but Sierra could tell when he wasn't wanted any more. "Sorry to bother you," he said.

At least he had a name now: Carson. He circulated around the room,

listening to the Sonoma people chatter about their business and their
retreat, the skiing adventures they'd had and the bedroom adventures,
in some cases. The Silver Flyer lounge, overlooking the main lobby, was
technically closed for the Sonoma gathering, but Sierra had dressed in his
nice clothes again and had walked right up the ornate staircase without
being challenged. He ordered a drink at the polished wood bar, and the
sheep just handed it to him. So he stuffed two dollars into the tip jar and
sipped his Manhattan. It was quite good.

At first he looked for coyotes, in vain. Then he just listened to
conversations around him with his phone to his ear, saying "go on"
or "I'm here" into the silent phone when people gave him odd looks.
By the time he'd circled the room four times, pretending to admire
the hundred-year-old pictures of the mountain and the famous people
who'd passed through Lonnegan's and the other things that used to
sit on this property, he had a basic idea of what Sonoma Systems did
(large-scale industrial automation), as well as which VP was sleeping
with which Director (both female, interestingly), but he had no better
idea of where to find Carmel-Carson, nor what relationship he had to
the company.

He had just about decided to give up when he caught the name
Stevenson, and perked his ears. "Oh, he left," a jackrabbit was saying, his
words a little slurred. "Wife took sick or something. See, that's why we
shouldn't be bringing wives along to these things."

His companion, a large elk, shrugged. "Ain't like we're going to Port
City. Where we gonna go to have a good time here?"

"There's places." The jackrabbit threw back the rest of his drink. "It's
inhibitin' my enjoyment of the full measure of this retreat."

"Not sure much is inhibiting you anymore." The elk took the
jackrabbit's glass. "Let me get you a water."

"Fuck water. The scotch is free, I'm having another."

"You've had enough."

Sierra moved away from their bickering. It was interesting, that
Stevenson's wife would have taken sick the night after Sierra'd seen her
husband with Carmel—if it had been Carmel. It certainly hadn't been
Mrs. Stevenson. He set down his drink, rubbed his chin, and walked up
to a group of four ladies talking, ones that had not been talking about the
business, two of whom wore name tags that started with "Mrs."

They paused when he approached, staring warily, so he gave them a
winning smile. "Oh my God," he said, "you all look so fabulous. And isn't

this room gorgeous? The paneling is real oak and the carpet is actually tasteful. When is the last time you came across that combination in a ski resort?"

That did the trick. The nearest to him, an ocelot, laughed, and the whole group smiled and relaxed. "Well, thank you. It is a step above their usual retreats, I will say."

"Seriously," said a female jackrabbit, whom Sierra suspected—given the dearth of other jackrabbits at the party—of being the wife of the inebriated one. "Did you all go with them on the golfing one two years ago?"

Groans bounced around the little group. "Golf and golf and more golf. And that dreadful kitchen," said the ocelot. "They served the steak with ketchup."

"I think it was for the fries," a mouse piped up.

"There was also A-1 steak sauce. Was that for the fries?"

"I like it on mine," the jackrabbit said. "And we don't eat steak."

"It's such a shame about Mrs. Stevenson," Sierra cut in. "I was sad to see her go."

"Hah." The jackrabbit took a drink.

The ocelot looked curiously at her. "I never heard what she came down with."

"Female trouble," the jackrabbit said, and the other ladies said, "oh," and the subject was dropped, but Sierra saw a sly grin on the jackrabbit's face, behind her drink.

"How did you know Vera?" the mouse asked Sierra.

He smiled at her. "Through a mutual friend. A coyote."

He kept one eye on the jackrabbit as he said this, and saw her startle, her eyes widening just a fraction. While the mouse asked Sierra about the Stevenson's lives, the jackrabbit looked down his chest and appeared to notice for the first time the absence of a name tag.

"Tell me," she said, cutting off the mouse. "Are you and this coyote partners?"

"In business, you mean?" He put on his best guileless expression.

She smiled back, tight-lipped. "Of course."

"Well, no. But I do find his business fascinating."

"I see." She took another drink and looked across the lounge at her husband for a moment, then turned away from Sierra and pointedly began talking to the ocelot about the treatment she'd had on her fur at the salon.

Only the mouse seemed interested in talking to him after that, and Sierra made polite conversation with her about the skiing on the mountain until he could pull himself away. He circled back around to the jackrabbit, wondering why his wife had looked at him after the mention of Carmel, but the jackrabbit and elk were only exchanging stories about clients they'd worked with, so Sierra moved on.

The gathering began to break up around then, with many people filtering down to the restaurant. He lingered as long as he could, dropping the name "Carson," but got no other reactions to it. So he stood at the thick wooden railing, set his empty drink glass on the polished wood in one of the rings that attested to the many people who'd done it before him, and leaned his elbows next to it. The trickle of people moving down the wide staircase to the restaurant had become a flood now, the kind of flood that wouldn't even notice one extra snow leopard. He had no doubt he could wrangle himself a meal, possibly free, but he had no desire to sit through another tedious conversation for five more minutes, let alone two hours.

Bret was no longer at the counter, which was good, because Sierra might have been tempted to ask him out for the night again, and that would have established a pattern. No, he would order something from room service and spend the night alone in his room, and if he wanted to, he could call up some porn on his laptop and jack off.

"I'll cash—catch up with you guys. Inside."

The loud words floated up from the base of the staircase. Sierra flicked his eyes down and saw the drunk jackrabbit waving his companions into the restaurant. "Tell Jenny ta save me a...ah, forget it. I'll sit wherever." He paced back and forth around the base of the stairs, then walked behind the curve of the staircase and out of sight.

Sierra left his empty glass and the empty lounge and paced over to the staircase, ears perked. He leaned against the large marble post and put one paw on the gold banister on the side where the jackrabbit had disappeared, staring toward the front entrance as though waiting for a friend, while he focused his ears down toward the shadows. He could just make out the jackrabbit's voice, muttering something, and just then a large group of people came in the front door, chattering loudly, drowning him out.

The people moved around the stair toward the elevator lobby and stayed there chattering away. Sierra sighed and walked slowly down one stair, then another, until he saw the tips of the jackrabbit's ears barely moving in the shadows to his right. He cocked his head, but still heard nothing.

He tapped his paw on the gold banister, claws retracted. One more step down. To his right, he now saw the corner of the registration desk. If he leaned over, he could see the couches and plush chairs of the main lobby of the hotel. Another step and he saw all the way down one of the hallways that led back to the rooms in the main building. And anyone in there—like the jackrabbit, leaning against the back of one of the chairs, could see him.

The jackrabbit wasn't looking his way, though. He was looking at the group of people taking the elevators. Another couple came in the front, but the jackrabbit didn't even turn. So he was waiting for someone, and not someone coming in from the outside.

Sierra's tail tip twitched, and his heart quickened. It couldn't be too much longer, if the jackrabbit expected to be in at dinner in short order. He gripped the banister and forced himself to wait patiently. Even if he were right about the jackrabbit meeting someone, odds were it was a female of some sort, from the way the guy'd been talking. It certainly didn't make sense that fifteen years of searching would end here in a remote resort in the mountains.

Although, in an odd sort of way, it did make sense.

The elevators dinged, behind Sierra. The jackrabbit perked up. "Hey," he said in the quiet lobby, and walked toward the elevator lobby—behind the staircase, beneath where Sierra stood.

Sierra cursed himself for watching the rabbit and not the elevators, and hurried over to the other side of the stairs, not caring how it looked to anyone watching. Footsteps click-clicked to meet the jackrabbit, hurrying behind the staircase before Sierra got to the banister. "You Stevenson's friend?" the jackrabbit said. Sierra barely heard him, and then only because he was listening.

This side of the stairs overlooked the front desk, where the caribou and a jackal were unoccupied. The caribou noticed Sierra and smiled up at him. Sierra nodded quickly and paused only for a moment before hurrying down the stairs as quietly as he could. He could walk around the left side, behind the staircase to the elevators, see who was there, and not be noticed. If he were lucky.

"He's a moron," he heard the jackrabbit say. "*I'll* be careful. Day after tomorrow, then." Claws clicked around the left side of the staircase, the side facing the restaurant. Sierra changed course, walking between the stairs and the front desk. Walking to the elevators now wouldn't take him behind the staircase, but he could turn his head quickly, and maybe he would even run into the person the jackrabbit had been meeting in the elevator lobby itself.

He got halfway across the floor and froze, staring. In the shadow of the staircase, a canid silhouette turned in his direction, and as it turned, a flash of gold in one ear caught the lobby lights.

Sierra could feel how conspicuous he was, like there was a big glowing sign over his head blinking DANGER DANGER. His lips parted, but he couldn't make himself say the name.

The coyote's eyes didn't linger on the snow leopard. He swept his gaze past Sierra as if he'd barely noticed him, and walked quickly away, out the other side of the staircase, following the jackrabbit.

Sierra's paralysis only lasted a second longer. He hurried under the staircase, past the plush armchairs and couches, in time to see the coyote walk past the host at the restaurant. He hurried up to the host stand and scanned the inside of the restaurant, but the coyote was nowhere to be seen.

"May I help you, sir?" the host said.

He recognized the vixen who'd seated him and Bret the previous night, but couldn't remember her name. "I was here with Bret," Sierra said, still searching the restaurant. All the patrons were seated, and the only people walking around were waiters. "I'm a friend of—I'm supposed to have dinner with that coyote that just walked in."

The vixen nodded and waved him through, losing interest in him. Sierra's tail brushed the host stand as he hurried into the restaurant, looking back and forth around the edges of the large room. Still, only waiters moved within his sight. He scanned the tables, but saw no large canid ears. No flashes of gold sparkled to catch his eye. "Excuse me," he said, turning to the vixen again. "Is there a bathroom?"

"Through the back, on your left," she said, without looking up.

He hurried to the back of the restaurant and turned, tail lashing in frustration, until he finally saw the discreet gold-lettered sign for the restrooms. He ran to the shadowy back hallway, pausing at the first door, with the male figure in a circle. The hallway bent around to the right, and the air back here felt colder. Sierra looked at the door again and then walked on down the corridor. If the coyote were in the bathroom, he'd have to leave, and the door opening would make a noise.

At the bend in the hallway, he turned. There, ten feet away, was a back door with a long aluminum pushbar and a glowing red EXIT sign over it.

Sierra crossed the ten feet quickly and pushed the door open.

Cold night air burst through onto his face. He squinted into the wind, blowing snow across the lonely paths that led to the Aspen and Birch buildings. A polar bear in a hotel uniform lumbered around the corner of one of the building, then disappeared around the next corner, leaving Sierra alone in the cold night.

If it were Carmel, why was he avoiding Sierra? Other than the fact that he'd been avoiding him for fifteen years. And if he were avoiding him, then why was he here when that article that had led Sierra to Lonnegan in the first place had been so obviously...obvious?

He checked the bathroom as a formality, but of course the coyote wasn't there either. One of the Sonoma people came in as he was leaving and nodded to him, but Sierra barely noticed. He padded to the door, lost in thought, and walked out into the cold, back to his room.

Once there, he called up the article again, the one that had sent him down this path in the first place. The "Tartok Ecole" header came up, and below it, the header: "Alumni Despatches." Sierra stared at the body of the article. "Lonnegan Ski Resort," it said, "in the Western Stony Mountains near Highbourne, is the closest thing to the slopes above Tartok that this alumnus has found in the world. 'It lacks only the cozy private lodges and their romantic fireplaces,' he says, 'to make me feel I am back at Tartok. The perfect place to take a leap, as Prince Charles reportedly did when he proposed to Princess Kelly here, when she was just a movie star.'"

The article did not credit the alumnus who'd written. Sierra had read it every night for a week after it had appeared in January. It was meant for him, he was sure, even though Carmel had many other ways of contacting him if he wanted to. He assumed the coyote did, anyway. Sierra had never taken the trouble to hide himself the way Carmel had; he still used his given name, he registered his car and put utilities in his name. He was easy to find.

1997: PRIVATE LODGE

Sierra was just putting his notebook into his shoulder bag as he walked out of Science class when Carmel came up behind him. Sierra's whiskers twitched, and he caught the familiar musky scent before the coyote said, "Hey."

"Hey."

"Girlfriend not around?"

"She took off to go get ready for tonight." Sierra hefted the bag over his shoulder.

"Ah, yes, tonight. The big dance party."

Sierra shrugged. "It's not that big a deal. It's just, like, this club, I guess."

"Forgive me," Carmel said, "but you don't seem like the dancing type."

The snow leopard smiled. "I can learn new things. I started skiing lessons this week."

Carmel's ears perked. "That's great. I just started a couple years ago. I thought, being a snow leopard, y'know…"

"That's partly why my parents sent me here," Sierra said. "Last year of school and it'd been about thirteen years since we lived near mountains. I don't even remember them."

"So your dad isn't stationed near mountains?" The coyote raised an eyebrow.

Sierra looked away from the query. "Well, uh. I can't go live with my dad. He's on a base, and there weren't really any good schools near him. So I said I wanted to learn to ski and they sent me here."

The coyote smiled broadly. "In a month or so, if you want to see some of the trails they don't let you on as a beginner, let me know. There's one that goes down into a little valley that's just gorgeous. Getting back out is kind of a bitch, but it's worth it."

"Yeah. Thing is…" The thought of going off somewhere alone with Carmel made Sierra's ears twitch and his heart beat a little faster. "Thing is, I kinda got into trouble at my last school for…"

They reached the exit of the school and Carmel held the door for Sierra. "For?"

Fresh, cool air filled Sierra's lungs. He breathed in deeply. "Well, it's not forbidden to go down there, right?"

Even after Sierra walked outside, Carmel didn't let the door close.

"Why'd you get in trouble at your school?"

Sierra looked back into the coyote's brown eyes and reached up to scratch his whiskers. "Went out of bounds."

"Uh-huh." Carmel let go of the door. It hissed slowly until a certain point, then the hydraulics released and it fell shut with a bang. "So listen, I happen to have a key to one of those cabins we were looking at the other day, the private ones on the ski trail. And I know that it's empty tonight."

"How did you get a key?"

The coyote smiled. "Why'd you get in trouble at your school?"

Sierra flushed again and scratched behind his ear. They walked together down the block, away from the school building and past the small stationery store on the corner. "Can we go tomorrow? You know I'm supposed to go to this dance tonight."

"I only have the key for tonight. You know, it's not a big deal. I just thought you might like to see what one of those looks like." Carmel swung his book bag from his left paw, back and forth like the pendulum of a clock. "It's so quiet when there's nobody around. Kind of feels like you own it."

"You've done it before?"

"Not with this cabin. Last year I found one that was unlocked. Sometimes they aren't too careful with how they secure their glass doors."

"Well," Sierra said, "maybe we can try one of the glass doors later in the weekend."

"Maybe." Carmel shrugged. "It's coming up on peak season, and the cabins are going to be full more often than not. If you really don't want to do it tonight, then you don't have to. I just thought it'd be fun. You can go dancing with your girlfriend."

"She's…" Sierra stopped. The sidewalks had gotten more crowded with people, so he stepped back out of the flow of pedestrian traffic into the entrance to a music store. The strong smell of the cheese shop next door filled the entrance, competing with the dusty chemical smell of CDs and the flick-flick of people shuffling through racks of disks. The clothing store they'd just passed showed tail accessories and ear hoops in its window that Natasha had been looking at the previous week. Sierra had the uneasy feeling that he was expected to buy them for her.

Natasha came with obligations; Carmel came with opportunities. He had told his parents about going to the club with Natasha, and though they weren't excited about him going to a club ("no drugs," they'd reminded him), they thought it was good for him to be spending time with Natasha.

His parents would not approve of Carmel, the kind of student who sat in the back of class, who thought nothing of humiliating a teacher (never mind how much M. Dupont deserved it), who was interested in spending time with Sierra one on one, not as an ornament to impress friends. But there was nothing illegal about going to spend time in a cabin, not if Carmel had a key.

Carmel turned and watched him, head tilted slightly to the side. "She's...what?"

"She's mostly going with her other friends," Sierra said. "I don't think she'd mind if I skipped out."

Whether or not Carmel sensed the lie, the coyote's smile didn't waver. "All right then. You need to drop stuff off at home?" Sierra nodded. "Cool. You know where the east entrance to the resort is, the one over by the lodges?"

"I think I can find it."

"Go to the *Teatro*." Carmel pointed down the boulevard, to the massive white marble theater building. "Take the Rue du Fleur, it's around the left hand side, and follow it up the hill. There'll be a sign there. I think the street is Rue Chambreau."

"Why don't we just meet at the *Teatro*?"

Carmel winked. "It's a little too close to your girlfriend's nightclub. Wouldn't want her to see us there together."

"I don't care," Sierra said.

"Perhaps not. But I wager she will." Carmel pulled a pocketwatch from his pants and flipped it open in his paw. "It's 4:30 now. Meet there at six?"

"Sure." Sierra checked his wristwatch, and when he looked up, Carmel had vanished. "Hey," he said, hurrying out into the street. "Should I bring...?"

The word "food" died on his lips. The crowd of pedestrians surged around him in the moist winter air. Carmel was nowhere to be seen.

His host family accepted his story that he'd be having dinner with Natasha. Calling Natasha to cancel was a little more difficult, but he told her he thought he was coming down with something and that his host family wouldn't let him go out in case he was really getting sick. She pouted, but told him to get better for Monday.

So he got to the *Teatro* at five to six, as the sinking sun was just beginning to lend a tinge of orange to the mountains above the city. He found the Rue du Fleur and followed it until he ran into a sign for the resort. The street wasn't named, but he hurried along it anyway, hoping it was the right one. There were no sidewalks, so he padded through two inches of snow along the side of the road, past row houses, and then uphill past a community park and a business park, past a strip mall, and finally to a small paved entrance with a sign over it saying, "Tartok Resort."

Carmel was nowhere in sight. Sierra waited for a car to pass, then walked up and through the entrance. On the other side, he found a paved path that he could trace, a black line through the white snow, uphill to where one brown log building, frosted with snow, marked the beginning of the lodges.

Sierra walked a little ways up the path, then turned to look at the entrance again. The road led to a small parking lot where a red brick welcome center and rental shop sold lift tickets; next to them, a small snack stand offered frites and baguette sandwiches. Maybe Carmel was waiting there?

He hurried back down the path and walked along the road to the parking lot.

"Hey, hold up," Carmel said behind him.

Sierra whirled, tail flipping around his legs. "Where did you come from?"

Carmel laughed. He stuck both paws in his jacket pockets. "That's a long, long story. Let's wait 'til we're in the lodge."

"I mean, just now."

"You hungry?" Carmel said. "Let's grab a sandwich before we go on up. They probably won't have food in the fridge."

"Uh…" Sierra's stomach growled. "Sure." He flattened his fur somewhat, though it stayed puffed up against the chilly air.

With baguette sandwiches of butter and ham in a brown paper bag, they walked together up along the path. Carmel talked about the resort and the famous people who'd stayed there. "It was founded by some fellow who made his fortune around the turn of the century in the frozen northlands, over on our side of the ocean. For a while in the twenties, there were a lot of diplomats coming here, and they actually had one meeting of the League of Nations here. After the war, it became a place where celebrities came. You know Princess Kelly? The raccoon?"

"Name sounds familiar," Sierra said.

"She was a movie star. Rent 'High Society' sometime."

"I saw 'Menace II Society.'"

Carmel turned and puffed a small "ha" of breath out at him when he saw Sierra was smiling. "Right. Different movie. Anyway, she came here one weekend like forty years ago, and for about twenty years after that, everyone came. Until the seventies."

They passed the first lodge, dark brown wood rising out of the white snow, dustings of white like ladder rungs in the crevices between the logs. Sierra looked in the window and saw, against the shadowed interior, chairs and a sofa of light wood with dark knots, polished so that even the faint light left in the sky created twisting reflections from it. No figures moved inside, but he saw bars of polished wood set above the floor. "Do bats live in that one?"

"Nobody lives in any of them," Carmel said. "But they made lots of species modifications in the seventies. There's a bunch that have warmed pools for aquatics."

"My best friend in sixth grade was a rat," Sierra said. "His house was dark all the time."

"They all have dimmer switches." Carmel turned his muzzle slightly as they rounded the corner of the cabin and a stiff breeze met them. His large ears folded back against his head. "Anyway, the seventies ruined everything. There were lots of drugs here and the place got a seedy reputation. Nobody wanted to come here until the late eighties, after Princess Kelly died, and then there was a TV movie about her that showed this resort and it got really popular. That's when the new money crowd descended on it. They don't even ski half the time. They just want to show off their money."

"Isn't that what celebrities do, too?"

Carmel turned while walking. "Celebrities appreciated the beauty of the location. The rich guys don't care about that. They just want to show off that they could afford the price tag. Didn't matter that they had the mountains, or the curtains, the custom-made furniture or the weather. They didn't care which cabin Princess Kelly slept in except that it was the most expensive."

Sierra curled his tail tip up as he walked. He felt like he should care more than he did. "Why do you care?"

Carmel didn't answer immediately. His tail swung behind him as they approached another cabin, this one also dark inside. Sierra smelled water and saw that all the windows of the cabin were translucent with steam.

"Because it's beautiful," he said finally. "We need to appreciate the beauty in this world before it goes away. Princess Kelly was beautiful, and this resort was beautiful, and the mountain is still beautiful." He stopped talking, turned to Sierra and stared at him.

In that moment, the golden light of sunset shone from the coyote's eyes, the effect bewitching. Then Carmel walked quickly on. Sierra shook the image from his mind and then hurried to follow. "The mountain is beautiful," he said quickly, and meant it, but Carmel remained silent until they'd passed one more cabin. Sierra turned, noting that he could just barely see the last one. "These are all so far apart," he said.

"Privacy." Carmel said. His ears came up slightly. "If you wanted to get adjacent cabins with someone, you could get from one to the other easily enough, but if you wanted to pretend nobody else was here with you, you could do that too. Though when Jallen Fox and Perrik DeLune stayed in adjacent cabins in 1977, supposedly they kept the path between the cabins better groomed than the resort staff did."

Sierra knew Jallen Fox, an actor he'd seen on late-night TV broadcasts of old 70s movies many times, but he'd never heard of Perrik DeLune. It sounded like they were both guys, and he wondered for the first time if Carmel meant to bring him to this private cabin for something other than just a night of chatting and drinking.

Perhaps it wasn't, strictly speaking, the first time he'd wondered. But Sierra'd dismissed those notions. After all, he'd never given Carmel any indication that he was interested in him.

Well, unless you counted canceling a date with his girlfriend to come on this evening with him. This date with him.

No, no. Not a date. Or was it?

He stopped on the trail. The coyote didn't notice at first, plowing on ahead, but a moment later he turned back to Sierra. "You okay?"

"Is this a date?" Sierra wanted to ask, but he also didn't want the coyote to think he was an idiot. What if it wasn't a date—of course it wasn't—and then Carmel was offended and canceled the whole thing? Sierra wanted to see inside the cabin now, wanted to see where the princess and the movie stars had slept all those years ago. And he wanted to spend more time with the coyote. Natasha and her friends knew things about the world, but they were all shallow things about current pop stars and teen movie actors and who was wearing what brand of shirt and using what brand of fur cleaner and a hundred other things Sierra had no interest in. Carmel's story about the resort had piqued his interest.

"Just trying to imagine sneaking around from one cabin to another," he said.

The coyote grinned. "Let's imagine it in the warmth of the cabin. You may have minus-20-rated fur, but I sure as hell don't. My ancestors came from Death Valley."

Sierra followed Carmel to the front door and waited while the coyote opened it. They hurried into a small, dark foyer with a spongy floor, where they wiped their feet. The air inside the cabin was a little chilly, though without the breeze, Sierra was quite comfortable.

Carmel turned on a light, adjusting the brightness to a medium level. "You can see okay?"

Prints hung on the walls, landscapes of the mountain and surrounding trees. Details appeared as Sierra's eyes adjusted to the light. "Yeah, I'm fine."

"Cool." Carmel padded into the cabin and dropped his paper bag on the wide wooden table, then knelt by the fireplace. He fiddled with a knob, and a small blue flame sprang to life amid the logs. "Gas fireplace," the coyote said, standing up. "One improvement they made to these cottages that I don't mind."

The six chairs around the dining room table appeared to be from three different sets. Carmel chose one of the two captain's chairs facing the broad window and gestured as Sierra followed him in. "Grab a seat."

The other captain's chair sat one seat away. Sierra pulled it out and sat down, setting his own paper bag on the table. Across from him, the open window showed the slope of the mountain, whose top vanished above the top of the window. The slopes glowed orange and purple with the last of the sunset, even where skiers had churned the snow into a stream of chaotic rapids tumbling down the mountain.

Carmel had already dumped his sandwich and frites out onto the polished wood surface. "Sorry we didn't time it better. Sunset's beautiful here. But we'll catch the end of it. I'm starving," he said. "You want something to drink?"

"Sure," Sierra said. "Like what? And the sunset's really pretty."

"Well, the cabin has liquor, water or coffee," the coyote said, and then winked. "But you happen to be in the company of an expert planner ahead." He withdrew two bottles of beer from a pocket inside his jacket. "Want one? I guarantee it's better than whatever you've had at the bar with the foxes."

In answer, Sierra reached out his paw. Carmel slid one of the bottles over to him, landing it right in the center of the snow leopard's pad. The label had a picture of a chalet surrounded by snow, and the name was something that Sierra could sound out but had no idea of the meaning of. He set the bottle down just as Carmel slid an opener over to him.

"Cheers," Carmel said, lifting his bottle as Sierra opened his own.

Sierra clinked his bottle against the coyote's. The beer was smooth and rich, malty with a sour aftertaste that wasn't unpleasant. "Nice," he said.

"It's got a lot of character." Carmel dug into his sandwich, and Sierra did too, biting into the crispy crust and soft interior, the salty ham and sweet butter. Silence reigned as they ate, and above them the mountain faded from brilliant rainbow to lilac to grey.

It was nice to be eating in quiet, taking in the surroundings with the food, and not having conversation forced on him. Sierra ate his frites one by one, licking his fingers every third or fourth one when the delicious grease built up enough, trying and failing to keep it off his fur.

Carmel devoured his food and threw the wrappers back into the paper bag. But he didn't talk while Sierra was still eating; he just sat there tipping the beer into his muzzle a little at a time. Only when Sierra finally crumpled his wrappers and placed them into the bag did Carmel finally speak.

"Good?"

"Good." Sierra pushed the bag away from him.

"Me, I'm still hungry. But there's snacks around the cabin. Crackers and shit. I'll get something a bit later. You full?"

Sierra nodded and lifted the beer. "This helps too."

"Course." Carmel grinned and tipped another drink past his lips, curling his tongue out to catch the drops on the end of his muzzle. "Sorry I only have the two. It'll be time for liquor later."

"It's okay." He didn't want to confess that he wasn't that used to alcohol, that after half a bottle of beer he was already floating a little. He gestured toward the window with the bottle. "Sunset was gorgeous."

"So different from the city and the school." Carmel turned his chair toward Sierra and leaned back, looking out at the now-monochromatic landscape. "Helps to get away from all that." He waved in the direction of the city. "Helps remind me that there's a world out there worth worrying about."

Though the words were very grand and important, they were said so casually that Sierra didn't catch their meaning at first. When he did, he smiled. "You worry about the world?"

"Someone has to."

"Don't your parents? They're diplomats or something, right?"

Carmel took another drink, licked his lips, and set the bottle down. He tapped it with his claws. "They think they can save the world by asking nicely, getting people to agree to things. But people will renege on agreements whenever it's convenient for them. It happens all the time."

"So how do you think they should save the world?"

The coyote's tongue lolled out of his muzzle as he laughed. "You've got to make them think it's in their best interests to do the right thing. Because it almost never is."

"So, trick them."

"Essentially." Carmel's claws moved to the tabletop, drumming a simple rhythm. "That's what I want to do."

"How?"

"Oh, I've got a number of ideas." The bushy tail stuck through the ribs of the back of the chair wagged. "When I graduate, I'm going back to the States to see which one of them works the best."

Sierra nodded, lifting his bottle to his muzzle. "So…did you just ask me up here to tell me how you're going to save the world? Recruit me?"

The coyote leaned one elbow on the table and cupped his cheek ruff in a paw. "Why do you think I asked you up here?"

"Um…" Again, Sierra pictured himself saying that he thought they were going to be on a date, and again pictured Carmel's reaction: angry, leaping to his feet, demanding that Sierra get the fuck out of this cabin, that he couldn't appreciate beauty and reduced everything to sex just like Natasha and the foxes. But their conversation was so normal that that image felt laughable. "I don't know," Sierra said. "Is this a date?"

Carmel's ears perked up, but otherwise the coyote's expression didn't change, carefully neutral. "Would you like it to be?"

"No," Sierra said quickly, and then said, "I mean, it's not that you're not attractive. It's just that I'm not…that's not…you know, I'm, uh…"

"Some of your classmates might say different," Carmel said. "About me being attractive, I mean."

"Oh, well, what do they know? You're good-looking."

Carmel lifted the beer and toasted Sierra. "Thank you. And likewise."

He didn't talk after that, just stared at Sierra, and Sierra looked back. "Um, if you don't mind me asking…are you?"

"Gay?" Carmel chuckled. "I suppose. I'm open to dating a girl. I've just never met one I've wanted to."

"So, you're bi but you don't like girls."

"I like girls fine. Marianne is actually very sweet when she's not trying so hard to be Gino's girlfriend. And Paula is really smart. To be honest, I haven't met many boys I'd like to date, either. I just find that they generally attach less importance to sex than girls do, so it's easier to have a quickie and not worry about the day after."

"I guess," Sierra said because he had to say something.

"What about you? Are you really into Natasha or are you just doing the species obligation dance?"

"No, it's not that. I do like her. It's different." He tried to figure out a way to describe his relationship with Natasha. "She's…"

"She's very determined, and she enjoys making people feel good by making them part of her group."

"That's…about right." Sierra nodded slowly.

"She also likes making people feel bad by keeping them out of her group."

"I don't…I'm not sure…"

"Oh, she doesn't do it very overtly, and you've only been here a month. I've been in this class for a couple years now. I may be biased by the fact that she doesn't like me."

"Apparently you painted Marianne's tail green?"

Carmel laughed. "Yes, I admit that there I underestimated her sense of humor. I thought she was going to this dance thing as a joke, when actually she was quite earnest about it."

"What else have you done, besides that and Monsieur Dupont's slides?"

The coyote just grinned, quiet. "I suppose that pulling you back to class did rather tip my cards, there."

"And how did you work those permission slips?"

"Oh, that's easy. I wrote them out before I came up to you in the hall. I always keep two or three in my pocket with my name on them; it was easy enough to add two more. Much as I was tempted to leave off Natasha's."

Sierra shook his head. "You sound like…like just the kind of kid my parents told me not to get mixed up with."

"Sounds like you got mixed up with them anyway." Carmel's eyes gleamed in the soft light, flickers of the gas fire reflected in them.

"That's why my parents had to tell me." Sierra extended his forefinger's claw and scraped it down the bottle label.

"Any particular kid?"

Sierra stared at the bottle. "Ringtail named Rey." He didn't want to tell the coyote about the things that hadn't gotten them into trouble, the things his parents hadn't known about. That wasn't anything serious, but if he told Carmel, the coyote would take it completely wrong. If and when Sierra decided he wanted to do that again, he…he would be the one to decide.

"Introduced you to the wrong crowd? The wrong activities?" Carmel put a finger beside his nose. "Your dad's military, right? Strict?"

He shrugged. "We did dumb kid stuff. What about you? Your father's a diplomat, right?"

"Well." Carmel rolled his eyes. "Mother's the real diplomat. Father's just got the title. Yes, he's with the embassy, the junior secretary of something or other." He waved a paw.

"Is that how you got the key to this place?"

Carmel just grinned at him. "Let's move over to the fire."

As the evening wore on, Sierra felt even more grownup and sophisticated, sitting in armchairs in front of the gas fire, even if they were using plastic cups to drink the rum Carmel had magically found. They talked about politics and world philosophy, about the other students in their class, and a little more about their parents, though they both stayed carefully on the surface of that topic.

By the time he was on his third glass of rum, Sierra felt a warm haze of well-being that stretched down his spine to his legs and his tail. He stretched out his feet to the fire and raised his arms over his head, then collapsed back into his chair, his head far lower than the headrest now.

"Does your tail do that often?" Carmel said curiously.

Sierra turned his head, looking down at the tip of his tail, which was flopping back and forth, curling like a restless snake. "When I'm mellow," he said.

"It's cute." Carmel grinned, and his own bushy tail twitched with what Sierra thought of in his canid friends as suppressed wagging.

"It's just a thing." Sierra grinned back, though. "You know, I didn't know what this was going to turn out to be."

"Oh?" Carmel slid down his chair to sit on the floor in front of it. Bright eyes glinted up at Sierra. "Then why'd you come? You had a date all lined up."

"I knew what that was going to be like." Sierra shrugged. "I don't know. This is different. You remind me a little of Rey. He was always pushing me to do cool stuff. He tried to teach me to dance."

"Hah." Carmel grinned. "Hopefully this has lived up to his example."

"Pretty nice, yeah." Sierra slid down to the floor, because he was heading that way anyway, and Carmel was already there. His butt landed on the carpeting with a soft thud, and his legs ended up pushed against the coyote's as he leaned back against the chair.

Carmel moved his legs back, but not all the way back. His foot still brushed Sierra's calf. Sierra didn't mind, though. It was comfortable and almost reassuring, in a way. He felt sleepy, and even when he noticed that Carmel's foot was moving gently, paw pads sliding back and forth along Sierra's calf, he didn't mind. It felt good, friendly, and his worry about Carmel's ulterior motives had been dissolved by the alcohol.

"So did you leave behind any broken hearts?" Carmel said, his tone light. "I'm guessing you don't still have a girlfriend, since you haven't objected to Natasha's claim on you."

"Nah." Sierra shook his head slowly. "I dated a little bit, but…nothing ever really clicked."

"Too bad." Carmel's foot kept moving.

"What about you?"

"Oh." The coyote's voice trailed off into the warm air. "A few here and there. Nothing serious."

Sierra nodded, and for a little while they talked about girlfriends. The conversation faltered, then trailed off into a warm silence.

And then Carmel leaned over and kissed him.

2012: MEETINGS

Sierra woke the next morning to bright sunshine and birdsong, with two leads in his head. He could go back to Bret and ask about Carson, but he didn't want to lean on the pine marten until he had more information. So he started off getting into the hotel's network, or attempting to. He called the hotel's management office from his cell phone posing as one of the front desk clerks, and managed to get a temporary password to get into the system. But once inside, he found an archaic data entry system and limited search capabilities that relied on codes he didn't know. He could probably figure it out with some web research, but knowing Carmel, the odds that he was registered under his own name or even his own species (coyotes could pass for any number of canids with the right makeup) were pretty slim, and the sunshine was making him restless to get outside. The snow gleamed enticingly and the warm, still air in the room felt stuffy.

Besides, though he suspected the jackrabbit would be less willing to talk to him, the skunk already had. Sierra had been planning what he was going to say about Carmel to try to get more info from the skunk. If he focused just on the coyote and less on the business, the skunk might be more inclined to cooperate. The jackrabbit would be a decent backup. So he closed his laptop and went skiing.

This morning, there were few people on the slopes, and all of them looked like serious skiing tourists. The business people might be sleeping in, or might be having a meeting. That was fine. The sun dazzled Sierra even with his goggles on, and the crisp, cool air invigorated him on every descent. He checked the restaurant about every half hour, ate there for lunch, and when he wore himself out in the early afternoon, grabbed a beer and sat on the patio. When he wasn't moving, the sun actually warmed him almost to the point of discomfort. He opened his jacket and brushed his tail through the well-trampled snow.

The mountain wasn't too dissimilar to Tartok, when it came down to it. The restaurant, a very States-typical bar and grill, bore no resemblance to the elegant mountain lounge at Tartok's base, but if he just looked up the slope past the pines, the jagged mountaintops against the ice-blue sky could almost be the same ones he'd spent that last few months of school with. He held a finger up and extended his claw. Almost a match.

He regretted not having gotten more skiing in on Tartok, but he supposed he'd had enough. Telling people he'd skied Tartok never failed to elicit jealous whistles or enthusiastic memories, and after all, he'd skied other slopes plenty in the intervening years.

His muscles ached pleasantly from the exertions; he would have to see about a massage or a soak in a hot tub tonight. He stretched out under the sun and closed his eyes.

He could tell when the business people came up. The noise level around him increased from a low murmur to a loud buzz. When he focused on words, he caught phrases like "bullshit presentation" and "terrible Powerpoint skills." So he opened his eyes and scanned the crowd for a pair of lime-green skis.

It was half an hour before they showed up. The skunk skied down the hill—he must have come up another lift—in the company of a raccoon, and both of them headed for the restaurant. The raccoon found an unoccupied table while the skunk clomped over to the bar to get drinks.

Sierra got up and hurried to get in line behind the skunk, casually, as though it had just occurred to him to get another beer. As the skunk got his order, Sierra said, "Oh, hi there. Forrest, right?"

The skunk turned and looked at him blankly. Sierra put on a winning smile. "From the reception last night. The deal with the coyote."

"Oh." The skunk's ears flicked back and his eyes narrowed. "Right. You talk to Carson again? I haven't seen him."

"Nah. I just wanted to let you ask me a few more questions. I realize I came up kinda out of nowhere last night and you didn't really have a chance to talk that much. So look, if there's anything I can answer for you before we start having longer discussions, just let me know."

The polar bear behind the counter handed the skunk's beers over, fizzing amber in clear plastic cups. "Look," Forrest said, taking one in each paw. "Thing is, Carson told me this was strictly a two-person deal. So until I hear from him, I don't really want to talk to you about it."

He turned and walked away. Sierra stood looking after him, watching as he walked back to the raccoon.

"Hey, buddy. You want something?"

The polar bear behind the counter stared at Sierra as he turned. "No," Sierra started to say, but then the guy behind him in line, wrapped in a bright blue down jacket, stepped in front of him.

"He'll have an Amstel and I'll have a Corona."

He talked in a high voice, instantly familiar. It wasn't quite the same voice Sierra had heard on the balcony two nights ago, but it was close enough that Sierra snapped his head around. In the cold air, it was hard to get a scent, and the guy was wrapped in a jacket and had a scarf across his long muzzle. His ears were under his hood and white plastic goggles concealed his eyes. But his tail hung free, a sandy brush whose black tip just brushed the mounds of snow.

The polar bear handed the beers over and the stranger slid him a twenty. "Keep it," he waved, and then gestured to Sierra. "Come on, let's sit over here and talk."

Sierra's fur prickled. He could hardly believe that this might be Carmel, the first time they'd been this close in fifteen years. The voice was not quite right, for one thing. But that tail, and the gait, and the size...he followed barely seeing the world around him. The sun's angle had shifted so that the snow above him was in shadow, the sun a haze in his eyes. He lowered his goggles again and followed the sandy brush tail through the maze of tables.

They sat at a table apart from everyone else, around the corner from the main patio in the shade of the building. Sierra's whiskers twitched with the cold, but he was comfortable.

The canid unwrapped his scarf to reveal a sandy muzzle and glossy black nose. "Look," he said, and his voice was lower now, definitely the voice he'd only heard in dreams and memories until two nights ago. "I need you to lay off the skunk for a couple days."

Sierra swallowed. His mouth was dry with more than just the mountain air, but he left his beer on the table. Slowly, he reached for his goggles and lifted them. His own eyes stared back at him from the shiny face of the canid's goggles. Large triangular ears perked under the hood.

This moment he'd played out in his mind a hundred, a thousand times. He'd played anger, hurt, forgiveness, desperation, determination, calm, and ice. And now that it was here, real, he felt numb. Sierra licked the cold from his lips and said, softly, "Carmel?"

For a moment, the tableau stayed frozen. Only the coyote's whiskers moved, brushed by the wind. His lips parted, but no sound came out, just a white puff of breath. Then he leaned closer and said, "Sí?"

Sierra nodded. Still Carmel didn't take his goggles off. He studied Sierra for a moment and then leaned back. "Shit. Here, of all places."

"You left me a clue." Carmel didn't react or respond. "In the alumni newsletter."

"Oh, good heavens. You got that?" The coyote laughed and shook his head. "Been doing that for years. I never thought...okay. Look, you're not running a game on the skunk, are you?"

"What? No. I was just looking for you."

"Okay." The coyote's pink tongue flashed at his lips, disappeared again. "Whatever you want, can it just wait until I close the thing with Forrest? I promise I won't run off. I just need to get this thing wrapped up. I've worked pretty hard on it."

"That's it?" Sierra stared. "Fifteen years and that's it, 'wait until I close the thing with Forrest'?"

Carmel sighed. White breath floated in front of his goggles before the breeze carried it off. "I promise, whatever you want from me...it's been long enough. I know better than to hope you've forgiven me. But just give me a couple days. I promise, it'll all be cleared up by the weekend."

"You've been running away from me for fifteen years. Suddenly you put a clue in a newsletter and now I'm supposed to trust you? Maybe I should just go tell Forrest that you're running a scam on him."

Carmel lowered his head. "You're right, you're right. You have no reason to trust me."

Sierra folded his arms on the table and leaned forward. "So let's talk now."

The coyote looked around, back toward the main patio. "How about if I bring you in on the Forrest thing? I could use another guy on it."

"Seriously?" Sierra shook his head. "You want to put off dealing with me and you're trying to get me into a game?"

"There's something in it for you. I'll split my take."

"You think I want money?"

"No." Carmel reached up to lift his goggles. Familiar brown eyes met Sierra's, wide and open. "I think you want answers. And if you want, I can give you the short version. I just have a lot of things to take care of this afternoon, and I don't want to short-change you."

"Just tell me why—" The last word hung in the air between them. Carmel waited patiently while Sierra fought to settle the chaotic thoughts in his head. The big 'why' at the hotel, but also why Carmel had avoided him since then, why he'd left a clue in the alumni newsletter now, why he was here sitting talking to Sierra now instead of running away...

"If it helps," Carmel said, "I'm sorry."

"Sorry!" Sierra exploded. "Sorry! For what? For abandoning me? For conning me into..." Again, the missteps of his life over the last fifteen years crowded in on him. "I looked for you for years!"

"I know." Carmel drew his paws together under his chin. "I want to

talk to you, I really do. I should've gone back then, but I was afraid…
and my parents were…" He sighed, a long exhale into the cold breeze.
"You see? There's a lot of things to explain. I'd rather do it inside where
it's comfortable, where we're not going to be interrupted."

"Near a fire?" Sierra said.

Carmel's lips twitched, a faint smile. "Ideally."

"Who's going to interrupt us here?"

"Forrest, maybe. More importantly, the air is killing my nose." He
pulled his scarf back up over it. "Look," he said, his voice muffled, "I'll
meet you tonight for a quick drink in the lounge upstairs from the main
lobby. You know where that is?"

Sierra nodded. "What time?"

"Eight. No, seven. Seven. And we'll have a long talk, I promise,
tomorrow night. Day after at the latest. It depends on how these things
go. Are you staying at the resort?"

Sierra arched his eyebrow. "You don't know?"

"I didn't know you were here until ten minutes ago."

"Yes, I'm at the resort. You can find out the room yourself, I'm sure."

The coyote tilted his muzzle. "Easier if you tell me."

"Well," Sierra said, getting up, "when did you ever make things easy
for me?" He left his beer untouched and clomped toward the skis through
the slushy snow. He had time enough for one or two more runs before
they started closing down the slopes.

Rushing down the mountain, wind streaming through his whiskers,
Sierra tried to convince himself that the last twenty minutes hadn't been
a dream, that he'd really been sitting with Carmel in the shade of the
Lonnegan Restaurant lodge and had himself voluntarily gotten up and
walked away. From Carmel Coyote. He laughed sharply, and icy air
seared his tongue. It might have been fifteen years, but Carmel still had
that effect on him, that fascination and instant trust.

The thing was…the thing was, that except for that one time, early
on, Carmel had never really lied to him, not outright. And the coyote
never did anything he didn't want to, rarely did anything that wasn't part
of a plan. He'd been surprised to see Sierra, but he'd put the ad in the
newsletter.

So Sierra would go to the lounge, wait there like a friend would, and
he would see if Carmel were still his friend. If that term still had any
meaning over a fifteen-year gap.

He slid to a stop at the base of the run and joined the line to go back up the lift, the same one where he'd first seen Carmel talking to the skunk. He craned his head, and yes, there was the skunk with the lime-green skis. It didn't look like he actually skied; at least, not more than was necessary to get down from where the beer was. Otherwise he'd be in line with Sierra and the other skiers trying to get the last few runs of the day in.

Carmel was nowhere to be seen. Worry gnawed at Sierra, that he should've just dragged the coyote down the mountain, forced an explanation out of him. Even though he knew he'd never been any good at forcing Carmel to do anything, even though he couldn't imagine how he'd force someone to accompany him down a mountain on skis, the thought still nagged at him. In the end, there was nothing for him to do but ski the last couple runs as the sun set behind the mountain, feeling the wind with his mind still elsewhere.

At seven, he sat in the lounge in his second-best outfit, a button-down shirt hanging open over a t-shirt tucked into his jeans. At five after seven, he reminded himself that Carmel was never on time anyway, for anything. At ten after seven, he told himself he was an idiot for trusting the coyote again, and renewed his vow to stop looking for him after this. He would enjoy his Manhattan, would enjoy the rest of his skiing holiday, and then he'd go off to the west coast and start his new life, coyote-free.

And at thirteen past seven, Carmel walked up with the skunk trailing behind him and said in a loud, artificial voice, "Kotrat, buddy, there you are!"

Kotrat? Sierra half-stood and stuck his paw out, trying to remember whether he'd ever given his name to Forrest. He didn't think he had. In any case, the skunk didn't seem to think anything was weird about the name. He just shook Sierra's paw with a genial smile. "Sorry about brushing you off, but you know, you don't just talk about shit like this with anyone, right?"

"I guess not." Sierra put on a smile, sliding easily into his naïve character. "I was just pretty excited there."

"We've all been there." The skunk laughed and sat down. "Shit, I remember my first stock investment. Almost wet myself, I was so excited." He grinned at Sierra. "I was seventeen. My dad let me pick a stock. It dropped a dollar the next day, I held on. A month later I sold it for half price, took the loss, and a year later it was three times what I'd paid." He tapped his head.

Sierra nodded. "I see what you mean." He folded his paws and looked at Carmel, who was now dressed in a slightly rumpled blue collared shirt, a yellow tie loose around his neck. Without the scarf and jacket around his face, the creep of white fur up the sides of his muzzle was more apparent, and a scar on his chin, subtle black under the thin white fur, was new. But the scent was as right as the voice, like stepping back in time. Sierra slid into his persona without knowing exactly where he was going, just a little thrill of danger at running a game with a partner for the first time in fifteen years. All he had was confidence, but that was all he needed. For now. "But this is bigger than just buying a stock, I think."

Forrest lowered his voice. "More money'n I had when I was seventeen, that's for damn sure!" He laughed again. "But I tell you what, I'd never have seen a sure thing like this when I was seventeen. Hell no."

"Now," Carmel said, "what did I say about using words like 'sure thing'? I mean, if it were a sure thing, a lot of other people might be getting pretty excited about it."

"Sure," Forrest said, "but a lot of other people wouldn't have those government documents."

Sierra's ears perked up. "Right," he said. "The documents were what intrigued me."

"They're preliminary," Carmel said. "Like I told you."

"Sure," the skunk said with a grin. "Look, what does this mean, having this second guy? I thought you said this was a done deal."

"More is always better," Carmel said. "I can sell you seventy-five percent, maybe. I mean, I'm already offering the shares at a third of what they're worth."

"So how does that work?" Forrest leaned forward. "I get to call the shots with the company, right?"

"Of course," Carmel said placatingly, but he curled his ears back. With a jolt he hid behind years of experience, Sierra recognized a signal they'd used a long time ago.

"Hey, wait," he said, adopting a belligerent tone and leaning forward. "So I don't even get a chance at a majority share?"

The coyote turned with a desperate air that the skunk probably thought was real. "Now, hold on," he said. "Majority share isn't all that important. You'll still make money."

Sierra let the skunk jump in to describe how important it was, and he didn't disappoint. "You told me the majority owner gets to set the price of the filters," Forrest said. "The whole profit depends on that. Not to mention the industry negotiations."

"Oh," Sierra said, bringing up his snide smile. "Like you have experience with industry negotiations."

Standard tactic: get the mark emotional. Forrest bristled. "Hey, you little—I was director of Biz Dev for two years. I'm VP of Client Services now. What's your qualifications? Born with a silver spoon in your muzzle?"

Sierra waved a paw loftily. "I can always get business advice from Daddy."

He saw the twitch of Carmel's grin. Forrest clenched a fist and turned back to the coyote, who immediately assumed his serious, semi-lost expression. "Listen," the skunk said. "We had a deal. Six-fifty for the majority stake."

Carmel held up his paws. "Well, er…that depends on how deeply Kotrat wants to get in."

"He's a punk kid," Forrest said. "You want to take the chance he'll ruin this opportunity?"

"I know business," Sierra said mildly.

"Yeah. I'm sure you do." Forrest patted the air in his direction without looking at him.

Carmel's eyes met Sierra's, and for a moment it was just as if they were back in high school. "You know what?" Sierra said. "I'm not sure I want to be in business with you."

"Right." Forrest leaned back, looking relieved. Carmel looked uncertain, but on the side of his muzzle that only Sierra could see, his whiskers twitched, just a bit.

Sierra let the moment drag on, let the smug smile grow across the skunk's face. Then he extended a paw across the table, picked up his drink, and looked right at Carmel. "How much to buy the whole thing? Forget majority stake, I want it all."

Carmel raised an eyebrow and then looked down at his phone. "Let me see."

Forrest gaped at him, then rounded on Sierra. "Who the hell do you think you are? This is my opportunity! You can't just waltz in here and take my deal away!"

"One point two million," Carmel said.

"It looks like I can if I can raise one point two million," Sierra said to Forrest. Carmel's ears had flicked back when he announced the number, which looked vaguely discouraging, so the snow leopard said, "It'll be tricky. I know I can get nine hundred, but that last three might take a little doing."

"No! Fuck the nine, fuck the last three. I thought you said seven-fifty would seal the deal!"

This last was to Carmel, who shrugged, his ears flat. "That's what you told me you could raise. Kotrat has access to more, so…"

"I can have a million on the table." Forrest stood and pounded the table with the flat of his paw. "Tomorrow."

The two other patrons in the lounge looked over at them. Carmel said, with just the right tone of apology, "Well, you didn't tell me that. Settle down. You know how this works, right? I have to take the best offer."

He gestured toward Sierra, but with the back of his paw. Sierra thought that looked like a "go away" gesture, so he got up. "Let me make a couple calls and see if I can get that last three hundred. Father should be in his office still."

As Forrest sat, Sierra stood. He took out his phone and held it to his ear, but didn't call anyone as he walked away.

1997: GAMES

"Sorry," Carmel said. The pink tip of his tongue showed between his lips when he closed his mouth. "I kinda wanted to do that for a while. It looked like you wouldn't mind too much."

"Look, I can't…I'm not…" Sierra's mind spun. "I'm with Natasha."

"Are you?"

"Yeah, I…" He paused.

Carmel sat back against his chair. "If you'd really rather be with her, then I won't stop you. I just thought I was picking up on something."

"No. I mean, I never had that in my mind…" Carmel couldn't help Sierra give his parents grandkids, or advance in the military—his father talked about how much the army needed good computer scientists. Not so much about how they needed gay soldiers.

But Carmel's kiss had been light, the musky male scent not as objectionable as Sierra'd imagined it might be. Not that he imagined that a lot. But it had been gentler than Natasha, more of a lover's kiss than a possessive kiss, and truthfully, he'd had more fun this one evening than he thought he'd had the whole previous month with Natasha. And Rey, Rey had never kissed him.

Carmel didn't look particularly guilty, nor, for that matter, repentant. He just smiled patiently as Sierra shook his head. "Well," Carmel said, "it was worth a try. And I still got to kiss you. I was worried you might slap me."

Again, Sierra shook his head. "No. I just…" The beer and the rum were convenient excuses for his confusion, but they weren't solely to blame.

Carmel held up a paw. "Say no more," he said.

"All right." Sierra sat forward, paws folded in his lap. His tail, stretched out behind him, twitched and curled.

They left the lodge a little after midnight. Carmel was ready to walk out the door with the empty bottles and paper bags still lying around the room, but Sierra made him clean them up. The coyote grinned the whole time, until they were out the door holding their bags of trash. "I tell you, the maid service will do it."

"You got keys to the place, so they'll know it's you."

"Well, ah." Carmel locked the door and grinned even wider. "Not if I get the key back by six a.m."

Sierra stared at him. "You stole it?"

"Borrowed. No harm done, right?" Carmel pocketed the key.

"No harm?" Sierra's breath was coming more quickly. He tried to control his panic. "I can't—I can't be here. We gotta get that key back!"

The coyote tilted his muzzle. "Nobody's even noticed it's gone," he said. "Nobody knows you're here but me."

Military boarding school…leaving Tartok just when he was getting his feet steady and making friends… "No, Jesus, I mean, we gotta go back and clean up, de-scent the place. I can't be here right now, I can't be involved in this. They'll kill me."

Carmel put a paw on his arm. "Steady," he said. "Breathe. The police won't—"

Sierra's first impulse was to pull away, but he looked into the coyote's eyes and saw concern there, and confidence. "Not the police. It's just, if I get in trouble—any kind of trouble—"

"You're not going to get in trouble," Carmel said. "I promise. The maid service comes first thing in the morning and they don't know who's supposed to be there. They just clean everything. We'll have the key back in plenty of time."

His voice remained low and calm, his eyes steady. Slowly, Sierra's breathing evened out. "You promise?"

"I promise you," the coyote said.

Sierra exhaled, a white cloud that hung between them for a moment and then vanished. "All right," he said. "All right. If you promise."

They walked back to the Rue du Fleur in silence, Sierra repeating to himself, *you won't get caught. They'll never know. Carmel promised.* He looked up the mountain, and now the lights of the snowmobiles made him flinch. Silly, he scolded himself, and then he smiled. Even if the snowmobiles did come after them, he and Carmel would have no trouble getting away. "If they see us," he whispered to Carmel as one snowmobile passed close to them, "they'll probably arrest us."

"No, they—" The coyote's eyes widened as they met Sierra's. His voice dropped conspiratorially. "You know, I think you're right. We'd better move silently as we can."

They padded quickly along the path, a little hunched over. At the last lodge before the gate, Carmel made a dramatic show of holding Sierra back while he checked the area, big ears flicking every which way, and then he crept slowly forward.

About fifty feet from the gate, a snowmobile headed their way. "Run!" Carmel called in a hoarse whisper. "They'll get us!" They dashed to the gate and through to emerge, laughing, on the other side. "Well," the coyote said. "There was a moment there when I wasn't sure we'd get out of there alive."

"I know!" Sierra grinned. "The lights were coming on fast."

"But we're faster." The coyote looked on up the street. "You want to get some coffee?"

"After you return the key."

The coyote grinned. "There's plenty of time. The coffee shops close before the lodge office opens."

"Carmel…"

"Trust me."

Sierra gave him a long look, then dug a paw into his pocket. "I'm out of money. Only have like a franc left."

"S'okay." Carmel's ears dropped to the side and then came back up. "If you're willing to follow my lead."

Sierra frowned. "I'm not stealing from a coffee shop."

"Good heavens, no." Carmel winked and rubbed his paws together. "No need for that. Come on."

The Main Street had shut down long before then, but across the way from the resort and half a mile through a maze of small, windy streets, Sierra heard music, faintly, and smelled coffee and pastries. "Ever been to the Latin Quarter?" Carmel asked, and when the snow leopard shook his head, the coyote laughed. "It's a great place. Usually don't work the shops here, but then, I usually don't get coffee, either."

They rounded a corner and stepped onto a narrow street whose snow-dusted sidewalks were lit with squares of light from the cafés and bars on either side. Shadows moved in the light, people's voices called out, and music flowed from more than one of the gathering-places. The scent of alcohol joined the coffee smell in Sierra's nostrils, stronger as they passed a bar called "Pollo Fumado."

"Come on," Carmel said. He led Sierra toward a small coffee shop, so quickly that Sierra barely read the name "Café Trevi" on the door before he was inside.

Only three other patrons lounged inside the shop. A pair of red squirrels sat talking, and at the front of the café, a lanky goat stared out the window. He didn't glance at Sierra and Carmel as they hurried along the wood floor past the small round black tables to the front counter.

"Remember," Carmel whispered as they approached the counter and the stoat behind it, "follow my lead." He put an arm around Sierra as the stoat looked up and said, more loudly, "There, there. Look, it'll be okay. We'll get some coffee in you."

It took Sierra a moment to figure out what Carmel was doing. "I, uh…" He sniffled theatrically and wiped his nose.

"Got dumped," Carmel said to the stoat. "I just found him in a bar. On the floor."

Sierra took a step and let his leg buckle. Carmel had to work to catch him, pulling him upright with firm, strong arms. The snow leopard leaned into the coyote. He'd been dumped? So he would have to act like that. What would someone in that position say? "I can't believe she dumped me," he said. "I've never been dumped."

"It's okay," Carmel said. "Hey, can we get a couple coffees?"

"Sure." The stoat rang up the purchase without reacting to their story. "Six francs."

Carmel propped Sierra up against the counter. "Steady there, *mon ami*," he said. "I'll get this."

The stoat filled two small ceramic cups while Carmel dug in his pockets. Sierra watched and then remembered he was supposed to be drunk and sad. He swayed a little at the counter as Carmel drew his paws out, empty. "*Merde*," he muttered. "I had it…"

Now the stoat was more interested. Carmel turned to Sierra and put on an apologetic smile. "Hey, ami, can you get this one?"

Sierra shook his head. "I spent all my money!" He turned to the stoat and said, "On rum!"

The stoat pulled the cups back. "Right," he said. "Well, when you come up with six francs, come on back and you can have your coffees."

"Come on," Carmel said. "Can't you see he's in a bad way?"

Sierra stumbled again, catching himself on the counter. The stoat looked up at him. "*Si*," he said. "So take him outside before he pukes on the floor."

Carmel took Sierra's paw. "All right," he said. "I can see there's no hope for the broken-hearted here."

"There's hope." The stoat poured coffee back into the pot. "Long as they have six francs."

"Capitalist! Fascist!" Carmel called as they stumbled outside.

Sierra collapsed against the wall beside the coffee shop, laughing. "I'm so sorry," he said. "I should've acted more drunk."

Carmel grinned. "No, no. More heartsick. And instead of 'I spent it all ON RUM,' you should say 'she took all my money.'"

"Oh, that's good! Can we try again?" Sierra lurched toward the Trevi Café door.

Carmel stopped him. "Not at the same place. Are you really drunk?"

Sierra doubled over laughing again. "No, no," he snorted. "I was just thinking…can you imagine if we went back in there?"

Carmel giggled. "He'd throw us out."

"*Unless you have six francs.*" Sierra tried to mock the stoat's voice.

"Which we don't, because we spent it—"

"ON RUM," they said together, and the cold air bit Sierra's lungs, he was laughing so hard. "Oh god," he said. "Why would I say that?"

"I don't know." Carmel was laughing just about as hard. "You were doing okay at following along."

Sierra's breath came in short gasps, and his words had to force themselves out through his throat. "I had no idea…what you were doing…and I had to think on my…on my feet."

"You did good!" Carmel took deep breaths, though giggles kept breaking through. "You just didn't put yourself in the story. You were trying to tell it."

"What do you mean?" Sierra kept his paws on his knees, sucking in breaths, getting better control of himself now.

Carmel's long muzzle stretched back. His black nose glistened, a foot from Sierra's. He spoke softly. "You have to imagine you were dumped. Instead of trying to think about what someone who was dumped would say, just imagine you are and say what comes naturally. Build the story in your head and you can sell it to anyone."

"I only had a minute to build it!" Sierra laughed. "You can't expect…"

Carmel was nodding. "You need to evaluate them quickly so you know the story they want to hear. Most people want their lives to be more interesting. But they won't believe just any old bullshit."

"Okay." Sierra sucked down cold air. He looked up at the coyote. "So what do I do?"

Carmel raised his eyebrows. "You try again. Come on."

He trotted off half a block down the street, and Sierra scrambled to follow, slipping on the slushy stone. "Wait, again?"

"Sure." Carmel turned as he walked. One brown eye gleamed back above his smile. "Unless you don't want to."

"Well…" Sierra didn't slow, but Carmel did, stopping just outside a small lit shop called "Café Borelli." The snow leopard peered inside: this café had only five small wooden tables and a one-person counter behind which a female panther stood wiping off the counter. It was a much less traditional café; this one looked like it catered to tourists from the States. Rather than the typical small ceramic cups that held highly potent local coffee, this one served café au lait in styrofoam cups. Near the door, loose pages from the International Tribune had been tossed, and a sign by the register indicated that they would accept dollars.

"Okay, so. You've just been dumped. She's going to be less sympathetic than a guy would be, because guys can relate, but she's a cat, so you've got some species sympathy going on. Think about how you'd feel if you came to school on Monday and Natasha said she didn't want to be your girlfriend."

Sierra thought, privately, that that was not a completely unlikely occurrence, especially if she found out where he'd actually gone. But he didn't really want to imagine it, because while it would upset him, he felt guilty at the amount of relief he'd feel. That wouldn't help him act dumped. Now, if Carmel would say at the end of the night that he found Sierra boring, that there weren't going to be any more adventures like this one…that thought grabbed at his chest, and though the pang passed, he held on to the memory of it. "Okay," he said.

"And lean on the 'how much I loved her' angle. Girls melt for that."

"You're sure this isn't illegal?"

Carmel grinned at him. "Relax, Sierra." He said the name deliberately, and Sierra did relax. "You're telling a little fib to get a free coffee. Nobody will tell your parents."

The coyote opened the door, and Sierra banished the little flush of shame he felt at the mention of his parents. He imagined himself drunk, having nothing to look forward to except going back to his host family's house, day after day of boring school and only Natasha—no, not even Natasha and the foxes. He stumbled in after Carmel and said, "What am I gonna do now?"

The panther looked up. Carmel turned and gave Sierra a little flick of his ears. It looked encouraging, so Sierra continued. "I mean, shit, she just leaves me a damn note? We had plans. We were supposed to—to go skiing tomorrow. What am I gonna do with her lift ticket now?"

"Just settle down," Carmel said. "We gotta get some coffee in you." He held up two fingers to the panther behind the counter. "Two, please."

"Sì." She took two cups down and smiled. "Five francs fifty. Dark, regular, or decaf?" She pointed to three pots of coffee behind her.

Again, Carmel dug in his pocket. This time, Sierra stumbled to the counter and looked at the panther. "You look kinda like her," he said.

The panther smiled. "I'm really sorry," she said, in accented English. She leaned in and he could smell her perfume. "Maybe she comes back."

"No," he said. "She's going off with Carlo." He hadn't said the name with enough venom, he thought. What if some mysterious Carlo appeared at school and Carmel liked him more than Sierra? "Carlo." He spat the word out.

"Ah, I'm sorry," Carmel said behind him. "When I got your call I ran out, must've forgotten my wallet. I hate to do this, but…"

Sierra shook his head. "S'okay," he said, and dug into his pocket. He took out his wallet and opened it, making a show of looking at the empty billfold. He reached in again and took out his lone one-franc coin. He held it in his paw and stared at it. "She took my money, too."

Carmel closed his paw over the one-franc piece, so gently that it made Sierra shiver. The coyote smiled at the panther. "I'm really sorry," he said. "I guess I just have to take him back home."

She fidgeted and nodded. Carmel tugged on Sierra's paw and made a small, small motion with his muzzle, toward the door. Sierra hung his head and turned to follow.

"Wait!" The panther smiled as they turned and filled the cups from one of the pots. "Is late. Go ahead, have some coffee. I need to make regular again anyway."

Carmel stepped forward as she emptied the pot into the second cup. "Thank you so much."

Sierra stayed at the counter as Carmel took the cups to a table. "Thank you," he said, trying to be as overemotional as he could, remembering how maudlin Rey had gotten when he'd been drunk. "Thank you *so much*."

"Aw." The panther smiled at him. "You're so welcome. Don't worry, you will find someone else."

"You think so?" Sierra sniffed theatrically, then turned to see Carmel waiting for him.

"Absolutely." She gave him a little wave as he left.

He joined Carmel at the table. "She was totally hitting on you," Carmel said. "Fake accent and all. In case you want to dump Natasha."

"Nah." Sierra's tail flicked back and forth. "I'm good. I'm real good."

"Don't act too good. You still have to sell the downcast. Hunch your shoulders. Don't give up the story just 'cause you got what you want, not 'til you're out. But get out as soon as you got what you want."

Sierra bowed his shoulders, inhaling the rich, dark coffee aroma. Carmel patted him on the back again, and let the paw linger a little longer. A friendly touch, comforting. Good for the story. And when Carmel took the paw away, Sierra felt its absence like the brief cold when the café door was opened.

"How's the coffee?" Carmel asked when they'd sipped it.

"Hot." Sierra cupped his chilled paws around it.

Carmel blew on his and sipped delicately, lapping with the end of his tongue. "Sweet?"

"Mine's black."

"I mean…" Carmel whispered. "Because it was free."

"Oh. Yeah." Sierra bit his lip to keep his smile from growing too wide and giving away their charade. His tail tip still flicked, but that could be interpreted as restlessness, and anyway his giddy energy at their success needed some outlet. "Does it always work?"

"Not always." Carmel lapped again, delicate little flicks of his canid tongue. "But more times now than it did a couple years ago."

"You're a coyote. Aren't people always watching out for it?"

"That's what makes it fun." Carmel grinned, and then immediately dropped the grin.

Sierra followed his lead right away. He prided himself on being a fast learner. "You ever try for more than coffee?"

The coyote blew on his coffee and took another sip. "Played for all kinds of things," he said.

"What's the most…" Sierra blew on his own coffee, searching for the right word. "The most expensive? The most valuable thing you ever tried to get for free?"

"Ah, I don't know." Carmel met Sierra's eyes, then turned to look outside into the snowy street, where a few people were staggering along together, singing loudly. "I got my parents to get me a season pass to Tartok so I could learn to ski."

"They sent you here and didn't want you to ski?"

The coyote rolled his eyes. "Mom's convinced I'll break my legs."

"Really?"

"Well, Dad's broken his leg twice and his arm once. And he's been skiing four times. So it's not entirely unreasonable."

Sierra smothered a laugh. "Your father can't ski?"

"He's quite good at falling." Carmel leaned back in his chair. "And he's charming. Mom hates when he goes to the hospital because she's always worried she'll catch him with a nurse giving him extra care. Male or female."

He met Sierra's eyes when he said that. Sierra felt the echo of the kiss on his lips, and then, to his surprise, a slight pang of regret that they hadn't stayed curled up in front of the fire. He flexed his fingers around his coffee cup and took another drink of the hot, bitter liquid. "So skiing lessons are pretty valuable, I guess."

"It's not really about that. It's just about getting around someone, if you see what I mean. Like, that panther over there thinks she did a good thing, giving you free coffee. Thinks she made your shitty night a little better."

"So really, we did her a favor."

"Uh-huh." Carmel looked her way and smiled. "It'd be better if she wanted to cheat us out of something."

"Why would she want to cheat us?" Sierra glanced back at the panther, then out to the street.

"Ah, she wouldn't. But like with Mr. Dupont, the best tricks are taking advantage of someone's greed or stupidity. If someone thinks they're taking you and you manage to take them…" Carmel grinned and exhaled across his coffee. "That's the best."

The smell of his breath filtered through Sierra's coffee came to the snow leopard's nose: musky and sweet. "How many people try to cheat you?"

Carmel smiled just a little at the corners of his mouth. "People are always trying to cheat you, one way or another. There's not always a good way to get back at them, but every now and then you get a good chance, and then you've got to take it."

"Like when?"

"Well…" The coyote rubbed his chin and looked into Sierra's eyes. "Like your parents. Dumping you here with that strict host family, no doubt hoping you'd straighten up and fly right, huh? Like what you did was so bad."

"It was pretty bad," Sierra said, and then clamped his muzzle shut. Carmel's ears were cupped all the way forward, as if he realized Sierra was about to spill a secret. Hell, he probably did realize. Sierra took a deep breath. "My parents aren't trying to cheat me," he said.

Carmel relaxed his ears back, but didn't look disappointed at the lack of a secret. "They're trying to get you to behave a certain way. And they're doing it in this clumsy sort of nineteen-fifties father-knows-best kind of way, rather than treating you like an adult. It'd be great if you could get something from them that looks like you're being a good little cub, then use it to break free, or be bad." He scratched his whiskers. "I don't know, really. I'll work on it."

"You don't have to," Sierra said, and took a drink of his coffee, feeling warm inside from more than the drink.

2012: OLD TRICKS

The skunk was leaning forward, shaking one fist, and even from a distance Sierra could hear him arguing that he'd been here first, that Carmel had no right to move this deal to someone else. He'd produced an iPad and slid his fingers along it alternately with jabbing blunt claws at its surface.

Sierra kept his phone to his ear, waiting for Carmel to look his way. From this distance, the coyote could have been eighteen again, sitting in a classroom or in a coffee shop in the mountains. He moved with the same economy of gestures, often keeping one paw hovering in the air, ready to lift a finger to make a point or sweep an objection away.

If he were reading the situation right, Carmel wanted him to push the skunk just a little higher. Or maybe he thought the million was enough. Sierra wasn't yet sure whether he should come back claiming he'd gotten the one point two or not. He was confident, though, that he remembered enough to be able to read Carmel's body language when the coyote looked up to make eye contact with him again. They'd run this one, or a variant of it, on Perrique the chamois, over some silly thing—midterm answers?—he couldn't even remember.

He kept murmuring into his phone in case the skunk was listening, keeping one eye on Carmel. The coyote had glanced his way, but not long enough to be significant. So Sierra flicked his tail around his ankles and waited until Carmel looked up, with just a tiny side-to-side shake of his head. Instinctively, Sierra echoed it, and got the ear-flick of acknowledgment he was waiting for. He set the phone back in his pocket and strode toward the table.

"Bad luck," he said as he approached. "Forgot Daddy's flying overseas tonight. He's on a plane, can't be reached. I talked to Henry in Finance and he can't approve it right now. But I can get an answer for you tomorrow."

"I suppose…" Carmel said. He turned to Forrest with a patient, questioning smile.

"I can put one million on the table right now. Look." The skunk turned his iPad around to show a spreadsheet that displayed a bunch of numbers in different rows. He tapped one cell that read $1,004,000.

Carmel looked up at Sierra, now giving him the apologetic look. "It's a good offer," he said, "and Forrest points out that I'd get to keep a little stake in the company. For sentimental reasons."

"I can do nine hundred." Sierra tried to put just the right note of pique into his voice. He wasn't sure it was enough, so he thought about how he'd felt when Carmel had appeared again, about the explanation he felt he was owed. "I was the one who raised the bid originally," he said. "You owe it to me."

"If you could just get more than a million," Carmel said.

"I can't believe you're going to work with him instead of me." Sierra did everything but stamp his foot. His tail twitched with real exasperation. "Just give me a day!"

"I really want to get this signed tonight." The coyote tapped the table. "Once those divorce papers are served, I can't get rid of them without half going to her. Maybe all of it. And fuck that. I'll sell them for half what they're worth."

The gleam of greed shone out of Forrest's eyes. Sierra kicked his chair, petulant, and stomped away down the stairs. He turned at the bottom and looked back up, resting one paw on the newel. He could just see Forrest, smiling now, and Carmel, and he waited until they got up and shook paws.

"Sierra?" He curled his ears back at the high voice as Bret came into view beside him, straightening his plain yellow collared shirt. "Hey, it is you! Having a good time skiing?"

"Yeah." At the top of the stairs, Carmel and the skunk appeared. Sierra backpedaled and tugged Bret along the side of the staircase, out of sight. "It's great," he said, his ears aimed back to listen to the two descending.

Bret glanced up at the stairs and then back at Sierra. "Hey," he said, whispering, "weren't you looking for a coyote? Is that him?"

"I think so. Maybe." Carmel and Forrest weren't talking about the deal anymore, just about the weather. Sierra refocused his attention on Bret. "But he's busy right now."

"I'll say he's busy." Bret laughed. "I don't know if that skunk has a wife, but that coyote was making out with a jackrabbit I *know* is married." He gestured around under the staircase. "Back there, just a few hours ago."

"Making out?" Sierra turned his head slightly to watch Carmel go into the restaurant with the skunk.

"Jackrabbit—what was his name, Sheen or something like that—had his paw right on the coyote's junk. Just toward the end. Almost down his pants. Then the coyote made him stop. Too bad." Bret grinned with false innocence. "I was sort of enjoying the show."

Sierra frowned. Carmel hadn't told him anything about a boyfriend. Hadn't told him really anything at all, for that matter. "Are you sure it was that coyote?"

"Pretty sure. Gold hoop in the ear." Bret patted Sierra's shoulder. "Guys fool around, you know? Doesn't have to mean anything." He cleared his throat, and the pat became a gentle squeeze. "Speaking of... you got plans for tonight?"

The snow leopard met the pine marten's hopeful brown eyes, and when he didn't respond right away, Bret said, "It's okay if you don't feel like it. I mean, I don't really have plans, so I'm just asking."

"Nah," Sierra said. His eyes slid to the shadow beneath the staircase. "I don't have plans. I'd love to have dinner."

They ordered room service. In between finishing the dinner—a chicken breast with apricot puree and green beans for Bret, a freshwater trout with almonds and mashed potatoes for Sierra—and starting on the rich-looking chocolate dessert, they shed their clothes and curled up on the bed together. Pleasantly full, Sierra let Bret tease him out of his sheath, and after stroking Sierra to hardness, Bret took the snow leopard's shaft into his muzzle and sucked eagerly at it until Sierra shuddered and gripped the sheets and came, moaning deep in his chest. Then it was Bret's turn, lying on his back while Sierra bobbed up and down on the pine marten's thick shaft. Bret came quickly, with squeaks and jerks of his sinuous body and hot splashes of musk on Sierra's tongue.

Sated, they sprawled naked on the bed and picked at the chocolate mousse. Sierra dabbed some chocolate on Bret's muzzle and then licked it off, and Bret dabbed some on Sierra's cock and bent to lick that off while the snow leopard squirmed. Then Bret used a code to order a free movie on the TV. "No gay porn," he said, "just straight. So here's a movie with Ford Flame instead."

But the movie wasn't all that good, even if the fox was hot, and after an hour, Sierra's mind wandered back to Carmel, the topic he'd been trying to avoid with a rich dinner and casual sex. What was Carmel doing with the jackrabbit? It couldn't be serious if the guy was married. Maybe Carmel was running some kind of con on him.

Or maybe it was just casual, the way Bret was lying with his paw on Sierra's stomach now, Maybe it was just a hookup he'd made here at the resort to blow off some steam, to not have to spend all the nights alone. Sierra sure hadn't been celibate since Carmel left, and he sure as hell didn't expect the coyote to have been.

Ford Flame had lost his shirt. He leaped bare-chested into the room where two raccoons were arguing over how to divide the money from the robbery they'd just pulled. The fox shot one in the knee and whirled to face the second, who refused to drop his gun. Ford shot him in the shoulder, spinning him around.

"Ah," Bret said. "Predictable scene. The second guy's just going to stand there and give him plenty of time to deal with the first."

"Uh-huh." Sierra was only half-watching the movie.

Ford Flame went offscreen, and Bret rolled out of bed. "Hey," Sierra said. "Where you going?"

"I've seen this movie a dozen times. That's his only shirtless scene. You believe it?" Bret bent to pick up his underwear and slacks. "You'd think they know that gay men are fans."

"You taking off?"

"Uh, yeah." The pine marten stopped with his briefs halfway up his legs, which was kind of cute. "That okay? I mean, I need to get a good night's sleep."

"Sure." Sierra waved lazily to him. "Thanks for hanging out for dinner and stuff."

Bret grinned, a sharp little grin. "If you're not busy with that coyote tomorrow night, hit me up. You got a good tongue and you appreciate food, miracle of miracles."

"Long history of it," the snow leopard said. "Hey, that jackrabbit, you said his name was 'Sheen'?"

"Yeah, think so. I'll tell you tomorrow morning for sure if you want." Bret paused and looked away, then down at the floor. "Can't tell you his room, though."

"That's fine. Thanks." Sierra watched the pine marten's rear wiggle as he pulled his pants up, making sure Bret saw him watching, even though he was thinking about Carmel again, about the coyote's long, bushy tail compared to Bret's short, fluffy one. It was a little worrisome that Bret already associated him with asking around after room numbers. He would have to stop using Bret as a source. For information, at least.

When the pine marten had gone, Sierra turned the movie off and sank back into the pillows. Beside him, his tail twitched. He kept seeing Carmel with the jackrabbit, juxtaposing the images because he'd never actually seen them together.

He rolled over onto his stomach, still on top of the covers, and shut his eyes against the room light. There was really no reason he should have assumed that Carmel would still have any feelings for him after all this time. He'd basically been trying obsessively to track him down just to ask if he ever had. What he hadn't expected was that the image of Carmel being groped by the jackrabbit would make Sierra's jaw tighten, his paws clench into fists, and his tail lash back and forth across the bed. And Bret's scent still hung over the bed, in the sheets, in Sierra's fur. How would that make Carmel feel?

Well, Sierra didn't know, because he couldn't ask. Maybe if he enlisted Carmel to play a confidence game on Bret, he'd find out. Did the coyote only like him as a partner in a game? He buried his muzzle in the pillow. That wouldn't be so bad, he thought, and hated himself for thinking it. But it had been fun, the back-and-forth, knowing each other's signals, getting the skunk to toss an extra, what, three hundred thousand on the table with barely any effort.

But then, they'd always worked together pretty well. Naturally, from the beginning.

1997: STORIES

When Sierra got close enough, he could hear Perrique's high, nasal voice. "I told you, sell your shit somewhere else."

"This is the real thing," Carmel protested. Sierra waited around the corner of the hallway at the entrance to the basement. Carmel and Perrique were standing in a small alcove at a closed classroom door, talking low, but the hall was quiet and he could hear them. They had perhaps another five or seven minutes until the end of the lunch period, so Carmel would have to hurry. Sierra's tail flicked against the locker until he realized it was making a metallic banging noise; then he stopped it.

"The only 'real thing' you ever sold was that Coca-Cola from 1980," Perrique said.

"Um," Carmel said, "I never—"

"I know!" the chamois snapped. "It was a joke."

"Ah." The coyote paused. "Well, I always did have trouble with Gallic humor. Nice bit of States history, though. Anyway, if you don't want these answers, I'm sure I can find someone who does."

That was Sierra's cue. Just as Perrique was saying, "Then perhaps you should," he walked around the corner. At a glance, he took in the scene: Carmel holding a folded piece of paper, the chamois's nose in the air, turning away.

"Oh, hey, Carmel, I was looking for you," Sierra said, keeping his voice low. "Is that for the history test? The last set you sold me got me a 98. How much for this one?"

"It's math," Carmel said, almost apologetically.

"Even better." Sierra fished in his pocket. "I've got twenty francs. That enough?"

Carmel had given him the twenty for the purposes of this charade. Perrique had stopped, as they'd hoped he would. With the small ear-flicks Carmel had taught Sierra to recognize, the coyote told him to slow his enthusiasm. "I guess it's enough," Carmel said.

"*Attends.*" Perrique held up a hand, blunt fingernails waving. "You used his tests? And succeeded?"

"Sure." Sierra smiled. He really had gotten a 98 on the history test, but had done it himself. He waved the twenty-franc note at Carmel. "Come on, I haven't studied for math at all."

Math—advanced geometry, specifically—was Perrique's weakest

subject. The chamois stared at the paper in Carmel's paw. "How do you know these to be the right answers?" he asked Sierra.

"I don't," Sierra said, and in fact he was pretty sure they were not. Carmel had taken the test from a posting he'd found the previous year and switched around some of the problems with homework problems they'd done so that it looked like a reasonable approximation of a test. "But I dunno, if it is, then why not? Twenty francs isn't so much."

To Perrique it wasn't, though to Sierra and Carmel, it definitely was. He only got ten each week as an allowance, and that was enough to force him to eat with his host family every night he couldn't get Natasha to pay for something—or, more recently, cadge a free meal somewhere with Carmel.

The chamois clearly was thinking along the same lines. "Une minute," he grumbled, fishing in the back of his wide jeans for his wallet.

Carmel flicked the black tip of his tail, the only sign of his glee he would permit himself. Sierra knew it now and hid his own grin.

And then. "Sierra! Are you talking to that coyote again?"

Natasha huffed around the corner behind him. "I swear," she said, "you should just date him or something."

They were careful at school not to talk too much, but Natasha was always somewhere around Sierra and so even though she only saw him about half the times he was talking to Carmel, she still saw twice as many as anyone else. Especially Perrique, who normally took as much notice of the snow leopards as he did the janitors, and who now froze, nostrils flared.

"Come on," Natasha said. "I want to show you this outfit I found."

"You and he are friends, eh?" Perrique looked between the two of them.

"I bought a test from him," Sierra started, but Natasha, now in the center of their little group, laughed and cut him off.

"Oh, I don't know if they're friends, but they're always planning something. I have to drag Sierra away before he gets into trouble. Now come *on*." Her high, girlish laugh was as false as Sierra's protested innocence. With a look at Carmel, he let her drag him away.

As they walked down the hall, back toward the main body of the school, he heard the chamois say, "No, I think I will keep my twenty."

Dammit. Sierra sent a silent apology back down toward Carmel. They'd worked all week on identifying the mark, practicing their patter— it wasn't complicated, but it had been fun, and now they were left with nothing.

Natasha opened a catalog to show him the dress she wanted to wear for the school dance the following month, and Sierra nodded dutifully, thinking about the twenty francs and Perrique again. He wondered if he could get into the school computers and find out anything about the upcoming tests.

"Sierra," Natasha said, and her tone had a sharp edge to it, much more serious than the gaily light voice in which she'd been talking about dresses. He looked up; they were alone in the stairwell that led to the second floor where their next class was.

"The dress is nice," he said.

She raised an eyebrow and closed the catalog. "Really. What color was it?"

"Um." She had flipped past so many dresses. "Blue."

"Sea green." She didn't open the catalog again. "You know, you're not being a very good boyfriend. It wasn't just that dance a month or so ago when you had a 'headache.' It was the restaurant two weeks ago, and then the movie last night."

"Oh," he said, but then couldn't think of anything else to say that wasn't an outright lie, or terribly rude.

"No, no," she said. "Don't deny it. It's all right if it doesn't work out. Father says I'll meet some real high-class snow leopards in college. But I want to give it a try. Come with me to the dance, that's all. Just let's stay together for the next month, and ideally until graduation."

"Um," he said. "Why?"

"Because you're nice, in a school full of self-absorbed nitwits. Because it looks good. Because otherwise I am going to have to ask someone else to the dance, and I don't have the time or energy for that. And because we're snow leopards and we should stick together. Even if you'd rather just play your stupid games with that low-class coyote. You can still come with me to the Valhalla concert if you want."

That was tempting; her father had gotten her a pair of tickets on the floor. He studied her and considered. Two months ago, he might've just said, "Sure," and let it go at that. But his time with Carmel had given him a different instinct. "Well," he said, "I'd hate for you to have to ask someone else to the dance. But me, I could just not go to the dance. I don't really care that much about it."

Her eyes darkened and her voice lowered. "You want to know what's in it for you, is that it?"

"I'm happy to help you out," he said.

She took his paw and pressed it to her right breast. "There," she said. "That's what's in it for you."

Beneath the thin fabric of her blouse, the breast was warm. Below his fingers, the hardness of her nipple grew. Sierra wasn't sure what to do. Should he just leave his paw there? Should he flex his fingers? He smiled—it had been a long time since he'd gotten to feel a breast—and then couldn't resist squeezing a little bit. His groin stirred, hardened, and his heart beat more quickly. Natasha's scent came to him, sexy and aroused, more so even than he was.

Her eyes met his, long enough to see the interest there, and she breathed in and out through her nose. Her muzzle curved in a small smile. "All right, all right." Natasha pulled his paw away. "You can do that every so often. And after the dance, maybe more." Her gaze traveled down his body.

"If there were any other snow leopards around…" he began, and saw her answer before he finished. "Right. So, sure. If you don't mind me hanging out with Carmel."

She exhaled so dramatically he thought she might pass out for a moment. "Just keep it quiet. Like you have been. I certainly don't want people talking about getting his fleas on me."

Sierra nodded. "Don't worry."

She pointed a finger at him. "And don't stand me up again."

After that first evening he'd spent with Carmel—the one he now thought of as "the evening with the kiss"—he'd tried not to skip out on too many dates with Natasha, but sometimes the two social calendars collided, and Carmel always won. "I'll try," he said.

"I've told Marianne that you get migraines." She tossed her head and flicked her tail tip, and had opened her mouth to say more, but the bell rang just then. "All right, let's go."

After school that day, sitting in the back corner of a café down the street from the school, he told Carmel he would have to go to the dance with Natasha. "I hope she's paying you," the coyote said.

"Not with money." Sierra could not restrain a grin.

Carmel raised an eyebrow. "You get to sleep with her? You know she's already slept with Gino."

"Gino's with Marianne. You mean Carlo?"

Carmel shook his head. "Gino. It was about two weeks before you showed up here. He cleaned up fine; he's a fox, he knows. But her...she smelled like him until after lunch. Then she smelled like spaghetti."

Sierra stared at him. "Has she slept with him since she's been going out with me?"

"Not that I've smelled." Carmel's nose twitched. "She hasn't slept with you either."

"I told you that."

"Yeah, but I know you weren't lying." Carmel grinned. "You should've held out for money. She'd have slept with you anyway."

"It wasn't my idea," Sierra said. "I would've just kept on going out with her."

"Why?"

"Well, um." He linked his paws behind his head. "I don't know. I guess it's easy. It stops other people from worrying about trying to date me, or wondering who I'm dating, and it's not a lot of work. And she's cute, and we have a good time, you know, some of the time."

"Some of the time."

Sierra's hackles bristled a bit. "Well, clearly I can't hang out with you during school hours. So what am I supposed to do? Why don't you, uh..." He'd been going to say "get a girlfriend," then remembered he should say, "get a boyfriend," and then he was worried that Carmel might say that he had one. Then he thought that was ridiculous, because he would know, and then he was worried that Carmel would suggest that he, Sierra, should be the coyote's boyfriend. Then, obscurely, he was worried that Carmel wouldn't. And by the time he'd sorted through all that, the moment for finishing his sentence had long passed.

"Why don't I...?" Carmel arched an eyebrow, and Sierra had the weird feeling that the coyote knew what he was thinking.

"Uh. Why don't you hang out with us more?"

The coyote laughed, with some yips. "Like your precious elite would allow that."

"I could talk to them."

Carmel shook his head. "I appreciate it, but I'd rather study than put up with that kind of snobbish conversation. No offense. You're a better fellow than I am to be able to sit through it."

"Course, if there were a cute coyote, right?"

"Maybe." Carmel brushed an ear back with his paw. "He'd have to be really cute, though. With a twitching tail tip."

Sierra squeezed his paws together. Thinking about two guys in a relationship together still made him feel weird, like when he'd brushed his paw over the electric fence when visiting his aunt in Newfoundland. Thinking about Carmel with another guy made him feel weird in a different way, one he didn't want to examine too closely. Because it was ridiculous, basically, and a little scary, and he had enough to worry about.

So he diverted the conversation to ask what the next game would be—Carmel called them "cons," but Sierra liked to think of them as games. They talked it out, the other conversation left aside, until it was time for both of them to go home to dinner. Carmel's family was not nearly as strict as Sierra's host family, but the housekeeper did keep regular dinnertimes. Not that Carmel often worried about making dinner, but it seemed that since he'd been friends with Sierra, he went home when the snow leopard did, and thus made it to dinner more regularly.

And after dinner, sometimes, they went to one of the hundreds of small cafes in the city and sometimes paid for coffee and pastries, sometimes cadged them from other customers. They rarely worked a clerk behind the counter again, because, as Carmel said, you wanted to be able to go back into a coffee shop more than once, and you couldn't always have just broken up with a girlfriend.

The coyote developed another game, one where they would pay for their coffee and pastries—and it had to be the right coffee, thick and dark, and the right pastries, the uniquely regional rolls of flaky pastry with praline and nut filling that Sierra didn't actually like all that much. "They make us look native," Carmel said, and indeed, if they sat down near some people who were obviously tourists and struck up a conversation, they more often than not got tipped the price of their coffee and pastries for whatever little bit of advice they gave, or whatever bit of history they told.

There were a lot of tourists, flush with money, happy to spread a little of it around. After the time Carmel told a pair of wombats that the café they were sitting in had been home to revolutionaries fifty years before, Sierra asked how he knew so much history.

"I have a good imagination," Carmel said, and winked.

"You made it up?"

"Most of it. The Siberian uprising was planned in this country, and some of the people undoubtedly stopped in that café." He paused. "If it was around then."

"Wait, wait…" They were walking back to their home neighborhood, two blocks from where they would have to go separate ways, and the air was moist with spring. Sierra stopped next to a flowering rhododendron bush, the scent sweet in his nostrils.

Carmel stopped and grinned. "What? That's worse than telling the clerk you just broke up?"

"It's different."

"It's a story. People want to hear a story. People with army-surplus coats and espresso coffee want to hear about the glorious people's revolutions."

"But…" Sierra sighed. "What if they check it in an encyclopaedia or something? I mean…"

"Not everything's in encyclopaedias."

"You can't just make up history."

The coyote raised his eyebrows, the grin gone. "People make up history all the time. Who started the first World War? Depends who you ask."

"It was that guy who got assassinated."

Carmel waved a paw. "Convenient excuse. The governments all played a confidence game on their people. They knew they were going to war. It was just a matter of when. Now the story they tell their people is that war was precipitated between two giant national powers because one crazy anarchist killed an archduke. Think about it. Does that really make sense? Or is it just a story they told people because it sounds better than the real reason?"

Whenever Sierra argued with Carmel like this, he felt out of his depth. It was one reason he'd started paying more attention in history class, but still, the coyote had a habit of reaching back into his mind and effortlessly pulling out a relevant fact that Sierra couldn't counter. "So what's the real reason?"

"How do I know?" Carmel shrugged. "I wasn't there. But I listen to Mom and Dad talk all the time, and I read the paper, and I see how often those things match up, or don't match up."

Sierra exhaled, and then drew in a breath sweet with floral scent. Before he could say anything, Carmel pointed at the rhododendron. "Like that," he said. "Smells nice, doesn't it?"

"Sure." Sierra frowned.

"No, it doesn't." Carmel drew aside the branches at the edge of the plant to show a small vine with dark leaves and white blossoms. "Clematis. That's what you smell. It smells nice but isn't as pretty as the rhododendron. So they plant it nearby and hide it, so you think the beautiful pink flowering bush is what you smell." He let the branches fall back. "People make up stories all the time. You just have to tell the story you want."

"That doesn't make it true."

The coyote smiled. "If enough people tell it, it does."

Sierra exhaled. He looked again at the pink flowers and then put his nose right up to one. The floral smell didn't get any stronger. He stepped back and looked at Carmel, whose fur was pale in the moonlight and whose eyes gleamed. "If we tell the same story," the coyote said, softly, "then we're making reality."

The snow leopard rubbed his paws together, and then smiled. "Well. If we're going to make reality, then there's more we can do."

And that's why Sierra started a web page, "History of Ginebra," where he and Carmel would write entries for every historical story they told. Each story received a section on the website, and when Sierra was feeling bored, he looked up some true stories about Ginebra to add, to give their made-up stories more weight. He showed Carmel the computer lab at the school—he wouldn't dare bring the coyote home—and sometimes they hid out there, inventing embellishments to their stories. Carmel latched on immediately to the idea of creating a false corroborating source for them, and contributed enthusiastically with inventive, plausible historical details. The most outlandish ones never got written down, but sent both Sierra and Carmel into fits of giggles.

He paid more attention in history class, and also when Carmel told stories to the tourists, and by the time spring's early bloom was fading, Sierra was telling some stories of his own. His grades in History improved enough that his parents remarked on them during their weekly phone call. He didn't tell them why he'd been studying, of course, just accepted their praise and said that he'd been inspired by the city and the people in it, and he thought about what Carmel had said about inventing reality. It was funny; whenever he thought too much about that, he thought back to the kiss, and had the strange electric-fence feeling and an urge to kiss him again. Especially when they were sitting in the computer lab, Sierra's paws on the keyboard, Carmel sitting right up close beside him, paws close enough to rest on Sierra's legs. More than once, their tails had brushed, and Carmel didn't seem to take any notice, but Sierra always felt funny and moved his tail out of the way after each brush.

It didn't matter, anyway, because he was with Natasha most of the time during school hours, and she'd given him enough enticement that he found his mind wandering to the feel of her breast at least as often as he thought about Carmel's kiss. Well, almost as often. But he never sat as close to her as he did to Carmel, only close enough to catch her alluring scent. So it was natural that Carmel sitting so close, when Sierra had been with Natasha all day thinking about her breasts, would get him thinking about the kiss. It was still getting him all confused, and he spent a fair amount of time sorting it out in his bedroom.

The bedroom was another problem. His host family, black wolves from the Rhine valley, had sharp noses. The first time he'd masturbated and left the tissues in his trash can, his host mother had informed him sharply that he would have to "curb his urges" while under their roof.

He'd been shocked and mortified. His parents had never said anything of the sort to him, and for weeks after that he hadn't known what to do. He'd jerked off in the boys' bathroom at school for a couple weeks, and then Carlo, with his sharp nose, had walked in one time when Sierra had almost finished, and Sierra'd stopped, paw on his aching shaft, holding in his climax and the distinctive musky smell. That had terrified him enough that he resorted to the shower at home. After the first time brought no recriminations from the sharp-nosed wolves, that became his default. He bought himself scented soap and washed the evidence down the drain very carefully, and over the spring months, whenever he touched himself, he thought about Natasha's breasts, imagining them without a shirt on top of them.

But every so often, the smell of Carmel crept in, musky coyote and thick, sweet rum, and a brush on his lips. The first time, Sierra forced his thoughts away, but when it happened again, he was too close to finishing, and he just let it happen. Afterwards, he just felt strange about it, not bad, and so the next week, when Carmel's lips passed across his mind again, he let them remain. As long as he thought about Natasha's breasts, too.

Of course, he'd been viewing pornography on his computer for the last many years, mostly snow leopard females at first, then females of all other species. After meeting Carmel, he'd looked for coyote females, and had found some good sites where they were being serviced by well-hung coyote guys. Of course, it was more the ladies he was interested in, the oversized breasts (Natasha's were much more reasonable) and the bare spot between their thighs, soft white fur and pink lips. But the members of the coyote males were intriguing too, especially the curious knot that formed at their base. Sometimes, when stroking himself in the shower, he imagined a knot like that at his own shaft's base, and that made his strokes firmer, the waves of pleasure more intense for a short time.

Spring came, and the dance grew closer. Sierra's life had settled into a comfortable routine of Natasha during school hours, Carmel after, and both of them during his showers. As the ski season wound down in March, he felt good about his progress on the slopes, and when April burst onto the school grounds with a magnificent thunderstorm, Natasha took him behind the main building of the school for some wet-furred groping and a kiss that nearly left him breathless. Their wet tails wound together and his heart was still pounding hard when he arrived at his host family's home. His host mother told him dinner would be ready in ten minutes and he should dry off, and he called as he ran up the stairs that he would be a little late because he needed to clean up in the shower.

Carmel noticed, the following day, sitting in the computer lab writing down a story they'd made up the previous weekend about the famous writer Cross, for a pair of literary-looking foxes. "You're all worked up," he said.

Sierra, who'd been thinking about Natasha every time he got a sniff of wet fur that day, started with a jerk. "Uh, yeah, well…"

The coyote leaned closer. "Come on, what gives?"

"Well, uh." Almost despite himself, Sierra's muzzle spread in a smile. "Natasha and I made out in the rain. She kissed me and I had a paw on her butt and she was pressing her chest against me."

Carmel's eyes narrowed. "Uh-*huh*," he said. "And where did she have her paws?"

"On my tail." Sierra's tail flicked.

"Well," Carmel said, and he put a paw right there on Sierra's thigh, warm and dry, and he squeezed lightly. "That's great. Maybe she really will put out like she says."

"Did you think she wouldn't?" Sierra was remembering Natasha, but it was the coyote's muzzle that was close to his now. His ears flicked back, but the computer room was empty; it was sunny and warm outside, and probably everyone was in the park or up at the lodge.

"I don't know." Carmel's brown eyes stayed fixed on Sierra's. "But you've been kind of edgy for a while and I thought it might be because she never let you touch her boob again." His paw's touch burned through Sierra's pants, through his fur, which had been shedding in clumps.

"No, I mean, she said, after the dance…"

"Right." Carmel nodded. "They say that. But she could just be telling you a story." His muzzle hovered six inches from Sierra's. The computer room was empty. His paw was on Sierra's leg. Reckless energy surged through Sierra, and he leaned forward and pressed his lips to Carmel's, much as he had kissed Natasha the previous day, without hesitation, with the certainty of the moment.

The coyote froze at first, only his paw tightening on Sierra's leg. Then, just as the snow leopard was pulling his muzzle away, Carmel lifted his other paw to the back of Sierra's head and pulled, shoving their muzzles together and licking at Sierra's lips, and then their tongues were sliding against each other.

The sensation was weird, the male scent overpowering while the slick canine tongue explored his muzzle, but it was arousing, too, as much as his chaster kisses with Natasha while his paw explored her rear. And Carmel's paw moved up his thigh as they kissed, getting closer to that spot that Sierra stared at when he looked at pictures on his computer.

He could let this happen right here. If he kept kissing, Carmel would reach up and touch his sheath and feel how hard he was, how warm, if the coyote couldn't smell it already. He reached out with one paw to hold the coyote's side, and his fingers felt the weight and solid male chest against them. He dropped his paw to Carmel's leg, then beyond, and found the brush of the coyote's tail.

Carmel's fingers reached the crease in his upper thigh, where his sheath pressed painfully against the fabric of his pants and his balls were squashed in a way that was uncomfortable but better than any position he could easily move into, seated as he was. And then they moved a little farther up.

Sierra jerked his head back, panting. Carmel's tongue snapped back as quickly as if on a spring, and the coyote's paw pulled back just as rapidly. "Sorry," the coyote said, his ears down. "Sorry. I got carried away."

He was panting too, his tongue moving back and forth across his lower teeth, and all Sierra could think about was the warmth of that tongue against his. So strange, so different, so *good*. He gulped and shook his head. "It was my fault. I, uh…"

"You were all worked up from Natasha. And I, you know, we did that one time…"

"I wanted to," Sierra said. He gulped again. "But. Uh."

Carmel was recovering some of his poise. "Yeah," he said. "Not here. Want to see if we can get into one of the lodges this weekend?"

"I've got the Valhalla concert with Natasha Saturday night."

"Friday night, then."

"Aren't they closed?"

"Until May, yeah. Doesn't mean we can't get in if we really want to."

"I dunno." The heat of the moment had passed, and Sierra wasn't sure now what he wanted. Carmel was talking about sex, he was pretty sure: both of them getting naked on the rug in front of the fire by the lodge and then, then, what?

"Don't have to. I know that dance is coming up in a couple weeks. But I'm good at cleaning up so there's no smell left." The coyote winked.

Sierra's ears warmed immediately. The hard-edged voice of his host mother came back to him, sending his eyes to the floor and his tail curling in on himself. "Uh, yeah," he said. "You know, maybe some other time, I guess…"

They sat in silence. He could feel Carmel's puzzlement, and he couldn't figure out how to explain the change in his own demeanor. After a short time, the coyote got up and walked to the door, and Sierra thought for a moment that he was going to leave.

But he only closed the door all the way and put a chair across it. At the dragging noise, Sierra looked up. Carmel met his eyes, coming back. "It won't stop anyone coming in," he said, "but it'll make a lot of noise. So look." He took Sierra's paw in both of his and held it. "I just want you to know I don't want you to do anything you don't want to do. I mean…" He laughed. "Obviously there's some things that I'd like to do, and that's independent of what you want. But I don't want to do them with you unless you want to do them too."

Sierra nodded. "What…what kinds of things?"

"Oh, I guess you can imagine."

The snow leopard looked up into Carmel's soft, brown eyes. "Tell me a story."

The coyote's eyes widened; his paws squeezed Sierra's. "Well, when I kiss you, it feels special. Better than anyone else. I really like being with you and I'd like to be with you in some other ways, too. I know you don't have a lot of experience and I get that you're a little unsure about guy-guy stuff. But I can walk you through that, I think. I can make it a little easier. I think you'd enjoy it, and I know I would." Carmel took a breath and lowered his voice. "I'm not asking for a commitment or anything. Just to explore some stuff. And you know, basically most of the stuff we'd do would be the same kind of thing you'd do with Natasha. Only I don't have boobs, but, you know, she doesn't have a cock."

The hard sounds of the word made Sierra flinch and then giggle despite himself, and he almost said, "Hyuh, you said 'cock.'" But Carmel was serious, and so he restrained the urge and nodded. "Like…what sort of stuff? I mean, just…with our paws?"

"Or our muzzles." The very tip of Carmel's tongue flashed across his lips. "I've done the uh, tail once. Definitely something that needs to be worked up to if you haven't spent a good portion of your youth shoving carrots and fur shampoo bottles up there."

"Holy shit, really?" Sierra pictured his fur shampoo bottle, which was about the width of his forearm. "My God."

"Female fur shampoo bottles." Carmel made an 'O' with his thumb and forefinger. "Look for the tall narrow ones. They'll almost always have rounded caps. They're not made that way by accident."

"Oh. Lion Christ, I thought…" Sierra laughed at himself and then couldn't stop. "My bottle is…and I was thinking…"

Carmel giggled, his paws tightening around the snow leopard's. "God, no. A carrot is a good place to start, but use a condom, and don't eat it afterwards."

"Oh, ew!"

"I told you."

The giggles faded; they looked at each other, and humor bridged the discomfort. "So, uh." Sierra said. "I don't know about shampoo bottles, but, um." His heart raced. Committing to something like this would be more than just saying the words, wasn't it? Words were just the story they told, no truth behind them save what the two of them chose to put there. Only later, if they wanted, would the two of them create the story that made the words real, and there would be the commitment. "Yeah. I guess. It'd be cool. To try."

Carmel's eyes lit up. His ears perked, and in the quiet room, the slow swish of his tail wagging sounded like a broom sweeping the linoleum tile. His paws gripped Sierra's. "Really?"

"Sure." Sierra's heart thudded against his ribs. The warmth and pressure of the coyote's paws wasn't uncomfortable; in fact, he wanted to leave his paw between them and lean forward for another kiss. But behind Carmel, he saw the door with the chair against it, and now there was the promise of another night soon to come. As enticing as Natasha was, Carmel wasn't requiring Sierra to go to a dance, to be a consort, basically. He liked Sierra absent his species and social status, and that made the prospect of spending a night with him even more dizzying. It wasn't that Sierra wasn't sure Carmel would have agreed, before today. It was that he wasn't sure he himself would have. But after the second kiss, and the third, the prospect felt more natural and more exciting, enough to have him hard in his pants just at the touch on his paws.

2012: NEW TRAILS

He woke hard in the morning and stroked himself lazily, piecing together his strategy for the day. The rush of skiing appealed to him, and the weather was supposed to hold for at least one more day, so he was going to have to spend time on the mountain. But there was also "Sheen" and Carmel to think about, and Sierra had an idea of how he was going to go about that. He didn't want to rely on Bret; the marten had been helpful, but when it came to illegal procedures, Bret was either going to balk or become an accomplice, and Sierra didn't really want that level of intimacy with him.

So he spent an hour and a half studying forums and websites until he felt comfortable with the basics of the hotel's registration system, and then he logged in again from his room. The first thing he did was search for Carmel Coyote, and for the name Carson, but of course neither search turned up any current guests, which he had predicted. Only two coyotes were listed as hotel guests, and they were a married couple—probably not something Carmel could fake. Knowing the coyote, he'd probably just come here planning on finding himself a room with a mark each night. And Sierra now knew the room he'd be staying in tonight.

So Sierra found his room and changed his name on it, and then searched for jackrabbits staying at the hotel. Only two rooms came up, and it was easy enough to figure out that the married couple named "Shiene" was the couple Bret had been talking about, on the second floor of the Pine building. Sierra added his real name to the room, double-checked his work against the web page, and logged out. And then he went to ski.

In the afternoon, the echo of the wind still rushing through his ears, he poked his head into the lobby. When he saw that Bret wasn't behind the counter, he stood in line.

The caribou helped him, as it happened. "Hi," he said. "Sorry, I lost my room key up on the slopes. Can I get another one?"

"Sure." She typed into her terminal and took his ID when he handed it to her. "Want me to re-key the room?"

"No, no. I'm staying with the Shienes and they'd have to come get their keys." He reached out and took the plastic card she handed him. "Thanks so much."

"No problem." She smiled widely at him and leaned forward to wink.

"You cheered up Bret quite a bit."

"He's sweet," Sierra said automatically, but the remark troubled him as he turned away. He'd hoped she wouldn't remember the two of them together. Now if she said something to Bret, she might mention that he was staying with the Shienes, and Bret would say that of course he wasn't, and then there could be trouble.

He chewed over what he might do about that all afternoon, having a cocktail in the lounge near the railing, where he could watch the comings and goings of the guests. He sat near the table where Forrest and Carmel had sealed their deal, because Carmel hadn't arranged a place to meet him, nor had the coyote gotten in touch in any way.

Around seven in the evening, he saw Bret wander into the lobby again. Sierra sank down a little in his chair, but the pine marten wasn't looking up. He tugged at the collar of his salmon pink shirt and smoothed down the fur behind his ears, loitering near the restaurant sign. Had Sierra made a date with him? He reviewed their last evening. No, Bret had been pretty anxious to get out. Twice with the same guy was probably his limit.

Not that Sierra had a problem with that. A few minutes later, his suspicions were confirmed as a tall white rat walked up dressed in a sleek evening jacket. Bret took one of the lapels of the jacket between two fingers and said something obviously complimentary; the rat touched Bret's nose affectionately and put an arm across his shoulders as they went into the restaurant.

It was hard to tell the rat's age visually, but he dressed and acted about fifteen years older than Sierra. And the evening jacket was a Tikane—probably a thousand bucks. So he'd pegged Bret's type pretty well: well-off tourist. Sierra took a sip of his cocktail and grinned. He hoped the rat was a bottom and Bret would get to be on top, but at least he was happy the pine marten was seeing regular action.

In this country, in this time, it was so much easier to be gay. How would he have acted if he'd met Carmel in this kind of environment? Would he have gone for it in that computer room, taken the coyote's paw and placed it square between his legs, seen where things went? The kiss in that computer room was the first time he'd taken the initiative to kiss another guy, and he still remembered the terror and excitement of it.

Kissing another guy was still fun, but it didn't have that thrill, not unless he was going to go down to Millenport or New Kestle or one of those Southern towns and try to hit on a guy. And as much as he liked a challenge, he didn't need one that badly. He liked crafting the story and getting away with it, and having an escape route.

Carmel had taught him that, to always have a way out. Sierra tapped his paw on the rail and looked out over the lobby, which had remained coyote-free for the entire hour and a half he'd been sitting above it. He wondered again if he'd just been used in a game, if Carmel was already on his way south, or north, or east, or west with his million dollars.

But if that were the case, he reminded himself, he was no worse off than when he'd shown up at the resort. That didn't stop his tail from twitching restlessly against the railing, because it was clearly untrue. He would be worse off, because he'd been so close, and all the memories had resurfaced, and with this new barrage of information about Carmel's life, he didn't think he'd be able to keep himself from searching again, if indeed the coyote had abandoned him.

1997: VALHALLA

Saturday night, the bus dropped Sierra and Natasha off outside the Stade Olympique, a large round stadium that was only about two-thirds the size of the baseball stadiums Sierra'd gone to back in the States. They were swept off the bus in a current of young people in Valhalla t-shirts, the smells of alcohol and marijuana thick in the air, along with the curious chemical "poppers" that made Sierra's nose itch.

The parking lot, a madhouse of black-shirted fans in eddies and currents streaming into the stadium, smelled amazingly as strong as the bus. Sierra kept hold of Natasha as they made their way through, one arm around her back. "I'm so excited," she said. "Floor seats!"

"You still have the tickets?" Sierra asked.

"Of course," she said.

His paw rested just above her hip, but as they had to squeeze through the outer gate, he had to walk behind her, so he placed his paws on either side of her hips. Her tail curled back around him and they pressed forward.

"I didn't know there were this many people in Ginebra," Sierra said.

"This is their only show in the whole country," Natasha said as they walked up to the gates, large iron grills in a beautiful brick arch over which Sierra counted five reliefs depicting Olympic winter sports. "How old is this place?" he asked.

"Oh, twenty years, I think," Natasha said carelessly.

The ticket-taker, an older vixen, made a 'tch' noise. "It will be fifty years old this next year," she said in accented English, beaming.

"It's not going to fall down," Natasha said. "Anyway, what's interesting is what's inside."

"Was it built for the second Olympics here?" Sierra asked the ticket-taker as she checked the people coming in behind him.

"Yes, sir." She flashed him a smile.

He did some mental calculations in his head. "Did you know that those Olympics were attended by more world leaders than any other?"

"Sierra," Natasha said. "Come on."

The vixen gave him a bright smile. "I did not know that, sir."

"Sure," Sierra said as Natasha dragged him off. "To celebrate the end of the war."

The stadium looked fifty years old inside, all bare stone and worn wood beams, and under the scents of all the people marching through the corridor, Sierra smelled earth and stone and the age of the wood. It was pretty cool, he thought, but he had little time to appreciate it. Natasha dragged him along past pictures on the walls of the old Olympics and other events that had been held there: track championships, concerts, grainy black-and-white pictures and bright seventies color behind glass. One picture showed several important-looking people at a podium. It would be funny, Sierra thought, if his made-up history turned out to be true.

There were no merchandise stalls here, no food service along the corridor. "Can we get a snack?" Sierra asked. "What about a shirt?"

"On the floor." Natasha slowed to check the signs, and then pushed on ahead. "They bring the food around in little carts in the aisles. And the shirts will be outside after."

The corridor was barely four people wide, so Sierra could see where there wouldn't be room to set up stands of any sort here. "We should've eaten before coming here."

"We would have," Natasha said, "if someone had gotten to the bus on time."

"I had things to do. Homework." Homework on his history website, to be precise.

"There's more to life than good grades," Natasha said, and it was just as she said it, turning into the small archway where a red-coated usher prepared to check their tickets, that a light paw fell on Sierra's shoulder.

"I couldn't agree more," came Carmel's smooth voice.

Sierra gaped, but it was really the coyote, his broad smile wider, if anything, than usual. He wore a pink collared shirt and had a small camera bag slung over his shoulder, resting on his hip just above the gold-stitched pocket in his dark blue jeans. Natasha, who had just let go of Sierra's paw to show her ticket to the red-coated sheep, snatched it back. "What are *you* doing here?" she snapped.

"Oh, I'm here to see Valhalla," Carmel said. "Same as you. Only..." He waved a couple pieces of brightly-colored cardboard in plastic sleeves. "I thought I might get a *little* closer."

The sheep leaned in past Natasha. "For backstage passes, sir, you want to go around to the crew entrance, just along the way."

Natasha's eyes widened. She pulled on Sierra's paw. "Come on, Sierra. It's some kind of trick."

Carmel shrugged and slid the passes into his back pocket. "I'm sorry I didn't get three," he said to Natasha. "You'd be welcome to come along if I had."

"I wouldn't come with you," she said. "I'd end up in jail or something."

"My dear," the coyote said, putting a paw to his chest, "I am offended you would think my imagination so lacking."

"Sierra, this is a guaranteed ticket that works," Natasha said, and used the ticket to point at Carmel. "He probably just…just talked his way in or something."

Sierra glanced at the usher, busy with other people, and then at Carmel. The coyote didn't have to say the words, not after all they'd done, but his amber eyes asked for Sierra's trust and confidence. He hesitated, and Natasha pulled once more on his paw.

"You wouldn't want to get in trouble, would you?" she said.

That got his attention. He turned to her, and she went on. "I just want you to get through this year," she said. "You can't go to the dance with me if you're in jail for falsifying backstage passes or something."

Carmel shook his head. "How little confidence you have in me," he said.

"Why do you want him so much?" Natasha demanded. "Why can't you just let me have one nice evening with him?"

"Why do you want him?" Carmel asked. "He's clearly not interested in being part of your boring society group."

"He's learning," Natasha said, "and it's better for him."

"And for you. You like straightening him out, don't you?"

Sierra cleared his throat. "I'm right here," he said.

"Yes," Natasha said. "And where are you going?"

If he went with Carmel, Natasha would be sure to tell him how wonderful the show had been from the floor. But if he went with Natasha, Carmel would have a story to tell him the next day.

He was fairly sure the backstage passes were fake, or at least inappropriately obtained, but he also knew that Carmel had some plan to get around it, that his aim was not just to get Sierra out of a date with Natasha. At least, he was pretty sure of that. Sure enough to let go of Natasha's paw.

"All right," she said. "Give me your ticket, then."

He raised an eyebrow. "Why? You can't use two."

"Maybe I'll call Marianne and see if she wants to come." She held her paw out.

"You just don't want me to come back if it goes wrong."

"Yes," she said. "That too. You're making a choice, and you have to live with it."

"Fine." He gave her the ticket.

She stuffed it into her pocket. "Don't think this gets you out of the dance," she said, and turned on her heel, long tail curving sinuously behind her as she swept past the usher and down to the floor.

Sierra favored Carmel with a smile. "No turning back now."

"Why are you going to the dance with her again?" the coyote said as he led Sierra back into the main hallway.

"I promised," Sierra said, because he didn't want to say that he was still somewhat interested in sleeping with her as well as with Carmel, even though he thought the coyote probably already knew that.

"Right, promises," Carmel said. He stopped by a garbage can and took the camera bag off his shoulder. Sierra expected him to open it, maybe take out a small badge or pin to use as a disguise, but the coyote just gave the whole bag to him. "Carry this," he said.

Sierra slid it over his shoulder. "What's in it?"

"Does it matter?" Carmel grinned.

So the bag was the prop, not the contents. "Are the passes fake or…"

"I think you can work it out," Carmel said as he set off again.

They weren't wearing the passes, so they were fake. But they'd been good enough to fool the usher. Unless…

They were within sight of the door marked "Crew Only" when Sierra said, in a low voice, "You paid the usher to say that about the passes."

"I really only needed to convince *her* that we really could go backstage." The "her" was clearly not the usher. "She's suspicious enough that without that, she would have given you a much harder time of it."

He reached out to the door handle. Sierra started to ask if he had a key, but the door opened easily. "Come on," Carmel said, and his tone changed noticeably as Sierra fell in behind him. "If we're late with this again, they'll have a fit."

Walking in behind him, Sierra saw a polar bear in a red uniform eyeing them suspiciously. Carmel made to walk right past him, but the bear held out a paw. "Passes?"

Carmel jerked a thumb back at Sierra. "He's got 'em."

His ears flicked in a certain way, but Sierra didn't even need to see it. "I don't have them," he said. "You said you had them."

"No." Carmel turned around. "You have 'em."

"Look," the bear rumbled with a German accent. "You cannot go farther without a pass."

Carmel pointed. "We're bringing important stuff to the band."

And Sierra understood, then. The bear turned to him, eyes finding the camera bag, and said, "You can leave it here…"

"Uh-uh." Sierra put a paw protectively over the bag. "Not this."

"What is it?" The bear still frowned suspiciously, but Sierra saw what Carmel had done: he had shifted the question from "who are you?" to "what is that?"—a much more easily answerable question. He didn't know what Carmel had intended, but they had had enough conversations about famous people using drugs that he had a pretty good guess.

"It's…" He paused, really trying to come up with how to describe it. "Recreational supplies."

The bear fidgeted. His eyes flicked from the camera bag up to Sierra, then over to Carmel. "Only takes one person to deliver, ja?"

"Oh," Carmel said. "I'm not delivering. I *am* a recreational supply."

His demeanor changed subtly; he angled his torso and put a paw on his hip. The bear's eyes widened, and then he started to shake his head. Carmel took a step closer and leaned into the guard.

The bear drew back a little, but not enough to avoid Carmel's muzzle as it approached his ear. The coyote whispered something, and then the bear took a step back.

"So?" Carmel said. He wore a patient, assured smile.

The bear spent a long time looking at him and then said a word in German. Carmel inclined his head, and his hips. The bear returned his attention to Sierra, who cupped an arm around the camera case just as though it contained thousands of dollars of drugs. "*Ja,*" the bear said finally. "All right, go, go."

They hurried down the corridor past him, keeping up the personas until they went through another door, and then they had to pause. Sierra looked right into Carmel's eyes. "You're a 'recreational supply'? What did you say to him?"

"Oh," Carmel said, "just told him what I was going to do and which member of the band I was going to do it to."

"You know their names? I thought you didn't like them."

The coyote smiled. "I do my research. Here, put these on. They won't fool anyone up close, but they're good enough for a casual look." He took the fake passes from his back pocket and handed one to Sierra.

"All right," Sierra said, "so where do we go now?"

"Follow the buzz of people." Carmel pointed.

Indeed, though there were not nearly as many people backstage as out in the hall, a constant stream moved from a larger open area that Sierra assumed was the stage back into a smaller network of tunnels. As Carmel led him through them, his tail flicked. It was all real. He was actually going to meet the cougar who sang "Carousel," the one who'd written those words he'd listened to a thousand times. He was going to be in the same room with the fox who made their guitars scream, with the otter who played the hell out of the drums.

Shit. What was he going to say to them?

Carmel grinned as they reached a well-lit hallway. He turned and put a paw to Sierra's shoulder. "Remember," he said. "Tell them a story."

A story? A story? The only story Sierra could think of was about the time his parents had decided to send him to a military boarding school, and he'd listened to "Carousel" until he decided to run away. They had found him at the bus station, but had been impressed enough at what he was willing to do to avoid military school that they gave him one more chance. So really, he thought, if not for that song, he wouldn't be here today.

That wasn't what Carmel meant, but it was all he could come up with. His tail lashed against the wall as they walked down the hall. In front of them, a large black wolf eased out of a doorway, closing it gently behind him. Carmel turned to Sierra and pointed to that door. "Your show," he said. "You're the fan."

It was amazing that nobody else had challenged them. But Carmel walked right up to the door and, bold as brass, knocked. Without waiting for an answer—or maybe his large ears had heard one Sierra'd missed— he opened it and walked in.

Sierra's mind was racing. He stared into the faces of the otter and fox as they looked up, bemused. He had been going to go with the drug story, but in a moment, he recognized the glazed look of someone whose mind was completely elsewhere without the aid of pharmaceuticals. Or perhaps they had already had some. At any rate, he realized that this was going to be easy, that they could tell the band nearly anything, and all they were worried about was that they were going to be playing in about ten minutes. "Hi," he said. "We're the fans who won that contest?"

The cougar, the lead singer, was staring into the mirror, his eyes blackened with makeup. He barely registered their presence. The fox just shrugged and went back to his guitar, tuning it and humming to himself. The otter, at least, smiled and stuck out a paw. "Welcome. You're from the States?"

"Yeah." Sierra stepped forward and grasped the otter's paw. He was holding the paw that beat the drums he could hear in his head even now. It was about three seconds before he realized that he was still holding it, and he let go, grinning. "Sorry. Big fan."

"Thanks," the otter said, turning to Carmel, and Carmel shook his paw and echoed, "Love your work on the drums. Reminds me of Gutberg."

"Thanks, dude," the otter said with a little more life. "He's a god, though. I just smack it around a bit. Look, sorry, they shouldn'ta brought you back right now. We're going on in a couple minutes."

"It's okay," Sierra said. "This is cool." He looked at the cougar, wondering if he dared say hi.

"Hey! Joey!" the otter yelled. "Turn 'round and say hi."

Meanwhile, Carmel had stepped close to the fox and said something, so softly that Sierra missed it. But the fox's ears perked up, and he gave Carmel a sidelong look. "Yeah," he said, "Well, maybe after the show if you stick around."

The cougar—Joey—turned around, his face looking hollow. He took in Sierra and Carmel with a look that was sharper than Sierra would have thought possible, as if all his focus was turned on them. "Hi," he said briefly. "Thanks for listening." Then he turned back again.

"Your song," Sierra said. "Carousel. It changed my life." He cringed. Good God, he sounded about twelve.

The cougar flicked his tail and said, "Thanks, cool," in an abstract way, like he'd already forgotten they were there.

But the otter patted Sierra on the hip. "S'okay," he said. "He appreciates it. Just not real good with people."

The door opened, and a buck looked through. "Five minutes, guys, come on. Who the hell are you?" That was to Sierra, and then Carmel.

The otter stood up. "They won a contest. They're gonna watch from backstage and then we'll see 'em after."

The buck's eyes narrowed. "Right," he said. "They can wait here a second while you get on stage, then I'll come take care of them."

"Cheers," the otter said, and the fox murmured something to Carmel. The cougar was the last to get up, and when he did, he took a deep breath and marched out the door without a word. The buck closed the door behind them.

"Holy shit," Sierra said in a whisper. "It worked."

Carmel looked quite pleased. "I told you."

"We should probably go now, though."

"Leave? In our moment of triumph?" Carmel recited the movie line with a smile.

"No, seriously." Sierra took one more look around, breathed in the smells of the room and the band members, looked at the pictures they'd put on the mirrors, the discarded clothes, the half-finished sandwich. "That tour manager looked pretty on-the-ball. Didn't you tell me to get out when you got what you want?"

"The contest was brilliant, by the way," Carmel said. "Exactly what they needed. They're famous. All kinds of shit gets thrust into their lives that they don't want. Look how used to it they were. I didn't realize they still did fan contests like that."

"All your research didn't turn that up?" Sierra elbowed him. "Hey, what are you doing?"

Carmel had picked up a guitar pick and held it to his nose. He slipped it into his pocket. "Souvenir for later. Just in case."

"In case...we go to jail?" Sierra edged toward the door.

"In case after the show turns out to be as interesting as promised."

Sierra stared. "I thought you were just saying that to get him to notice you."

The coyote shrugged. "Probably nothing will happen. But you know, if the opportunity presents itself."

"Seriously?"

He could not tell whether Carmel was playing or not. The coyote just kept giving him that grin, and as easy as the band members and tour manager had been to read, Sierra could not penetrate that long, sly muzzle. "Fine," he said. "Let's just go."

Outside, the faint noise of an audience clapping rhythmically to demand the appearance of their heroes came to their ears. Carmel flicked his forward. "Just relax. We have a show to see."

The door opened. The tour manager stood there with the polar bear guard behind him. "Now, boys," the buck said, "let's see those passes."

The office of the head of security was small, searingly bright, and smelled strongly of badger, the main reason for that being the large badger behind the desk. Muscles bulged out of his uniform, and Sierra thought he took great pains to keep his arms flexed for just that reason. Even as he picked up the phone, he kept his arm bent at a ninety-degree angle.

The polar bear took up a good ten percent of the rest of the room, the tour manager beside him. They stood on either side of Sierra and Carmel in front of the badger's desk. Sierra's mind raced to figure out how to get around the security guy—flatter his muscles, flatter his authority—but there was also the tour manager to deal with and he was having trouble thinking, because he was mostly playing in his head the phone call from his parents that would come later that night.

He didn't want to do that; it certainly wasn't helpful in their current situation. But his mind was drawn to it. Whenever he started a dialogue in his head with the badger, like "it was a harmless prank, we never meant to do anything to cross you," it was his parents who answered with, "did you not know that lying to get backstage with fake passes was wrong?" And that inevitably led to registration in military school and leaving Tartok.

What was more, the bag Carmel had given him, with its unknown contents, weighed far more on his mind than his hip. Besides all that, he could hear some of the concert going on. Every five minutes or so he was distracted trying to figure out what song the band had started, and every five minutes he was frustrated because all he could hear was the throb of drums, and the guitar notes pounded together into an indecipherable wail.

"I really don't think the police need to be involved," Carmel said smoothly.

The badger held the phone, one finger still pressing buttons. "I do not believe you are the person to decide that."

Carmel turned to the tour manager. "You're right," he said. "Mister…"

The buck hadn't given them his name. Now, in response to Carmel's inclined head and politely perked ears, he said, "Gerhard."

"Mister Gerhard is the one who should decide it." Carmel said with a smile. Sierra glanced behind him, at the tight curl of the coyote's tail, and saw the black tip vibrating, the only indication that Carmel was at all nervous. Given how much the coyote usually let on, Carmel must be scared indeed.

"I already decided it," Mister Gerhard said. "When I told Monsieur Villiers to call them."

"But I think you have not considered all the consequences." There was a slight quaver in his voice, too. Hopefully only Sierra noticed it.

"Let's see," Gerhard said. "The police come, they take you to jail for trespassing. What am I missing?"

"The part where the charges against us are filed into public court," Carmel said. "Here in Ginebra, there's a thing called 'privilege' where someone who has charges brought against him may choose to have them heard in public court, and then any statement he makes will be entered into the public record. Newspapers and all."

The buck looked toward the badger, who hesitated, and then nodded. Sierra wasn't familiar with Ginebran law, but it sounded plausible enough. Gerhard frowned. "I'm not seeing a problem with that."

"Well," Carmel turned to the polar bear. "I imagine Mister…"

"Weiss."

"Herr Weiss here will be called to testify to the charges. Being the one who admitted us and all. And I would have to admit that I told him that I entered with the intention of performing certain sexual acts with a certain member of the band."

The entire room turned to stare at Herr Weiss, who looked distinctly ill at ease under the scrutiny. Clearly, Sierra thought, he had never envisioned his job including testifying in court to his role in facilitating unspeakable gay sexual acts for a famous musician. Outside, the crowd roared, and a new song started up with a soaring guitar solo. Sierra thought about Dvarjan, the guitarist, and about Carmel, and then about the two of them together, and he shut that line of imagination off.

"I don't see why that would have to come up," Mister Gerhard said, when Weiss failed to confirm or deny Carmel's statement, or actually make any kind of sound whatsoever.

Carmel shrugged, almost apologetically. "I would also have to include in my statement that I actually proposed that…activity…and that I was told to meet the band backstage after the show."

"I saw that," Sierra said.

"Jesus," Gerhard said.

"And Herr Weiss's testimony, that he thought this a reasonable reason to allow me entry, would establish a pattern of such behavior. Might not play too well to the band's image."

Gerhard tapped his thick fingers on the badger's desk. "I don't think it would hurt that much. Any publicity is good publicity. There are already rumors online."

"There are a lot of teenaged girls who love him," Sierra said, having regained some of his composure. Carmel had given him an idea.

"They'll get over it," Gerhard said. "Think they can change him, or something."

"Perhaps," Sierra said. He took a deep breath and caught Carmel's amber, encouraging eye. "But it might not play too well to find out that the band arrested a couple of lifelong fans who only wanted to get backstage and meet them."

Gerhard's fingers stopped their tapping. Carmel stepped in. "What I think it comes down to," he said, "is that we're really very sorry. We love Valhalla and their music, and this meant a lot to us. We're willing to go on home and promise not to do this again."

The badger and polar bear both looked at Gerhard. The buck's gaze lowered, to Sierra's camera bag. He pointed. "Open that up."

Sierra met Carmel's eyes, and the coyote gave him a quick flick of the ears, forward, then back. Encouragement. So the snow leopard fought his misgivings, reached down to his side, and pulled the Velcro flap up.

The buck leaned over, almost catching Sierra's arm with his antlers. Sierra glanced down, trying to look interested more in Gerhard's reaction than in what was in the case. He saw a neat array of a dozen plastic grey circles, the tops of film canisters.

Gerhard took one out, shook it, and then opened it. He sniffed the inside, turned it upside down, and then met Sierra's eyes. He picked out another canister and opened it, then picked up three more and shook them without opening them. "You brought twelve empty containers?"

Sierra shrugged. "They were props."

The buck dropped the canisters back in the camera bag. As Sierra closed the flap, Gerhard said, "Fine. Get out of here, and if I catch you backstage with the band without appropriate passes again..."

"You won't," Carmel said. "Promise." He grabbed Sierra's paw, and pulled him out of the office to thunderous applause from the stadium.

"You almost got us tossed in jail," Sierra said as they walked to the bus.

"They weren't going to throw us in jail," Carmel said. "They were just trying to scare us."

"And you were going to...to do something with Dvarjan."

"Probably not."

"Probably not?"

"Well, there'd be other groupies there after the show. No privacy. He might've taken me back to the hotel, though."

Sierra stared at the coyote, and Carmel grinned back. The snow leopard tried to work out in his head how the conversation would go if he said, "But you're there with me, and we agreed to...maybe do something like that...at some unspecified point in the future..." Carmel would look at him patiently and he would maybe ask, if you had the chance to—Sierra filled in a roulette wheel of sex acts here—with the guitarist from your favorite band… He would let that hang, and Sierra might say, but they're not *your* favorite band, and no, there the conversation was derailed from the point. He could try with, "but you would just leave me there alone?" but then the implication might be that he was asking to be included. And if he said, "but we were there together," then Carmel would infer that Sierra didn't want him doing—the roulette wheel slowed, ticking past images in his imagination—with other people. And that was more commitment than he was comfortable with.

He kicked at the ground. "You almost got us arrested," he said. "That would've been it. I would've been in a military academy before you could turn around. You want that?"

He hoped Carmel would reach out, would say, "of course not," but the coyote only shook his head. "No risk, no reward," he said. "You got to meet Valhalla tonight."

The bus pulled up next to them. Sierra remembered the feel of the otter's paw in his. "Yeah," he said over his shoulder. "But then we didn't get out."

And Carmel smiled and said, "Who said that was the end of the game?"

2012: PROMISES

Around 7:30, a voice behind Sierra made him jump. "When have you ever known me to come in the front door?"

He turned and saw Carmel sitting at the table behind him, grinning. Sierra's worries melted, and he reached out to hug the coyote across their chairs. "So I figured out what I want to ask you first. What were you doing with Stevenson?"

Carmel twisted awkwardly, not into the hug, but not out of it either. His muzzle was still; he was good at concealing surprise, though. "You know him?"

"I saw you on the balcony. Went to talk to him the next morning, but he'd checked out."

The coyote nodded. "Listen," he said. "I've got a few more things to take care of before I can leave. I told you, tomorrow night I'll be able to talk about all of this. Right now…"

He sighed. Sierra looked at the flattening ears, the curled tail. He tapped the armrest of his chair. "I guess I shouldn't be surprised that you've got more than one thing going on," he said. "You got your money from the skunk okay?"

"Yeah, that's done." Carmel glanced around. "Though it'd be good if he didn't see me around too much. You too, for that matter."

"You didn't want me to see you around too much?"

Carmel smiled. "I don't think he should see you too much."

Sierra stared down at his drink. Carmel was fidgeting like he wanted to leave. "I can help with this other thing, too, maybe."

"Um. No, I can't use you on this thing." He wouldn't meet Sierra's eyes.

"Why don't you use your boyfriend?"

Carmel's eyes widened. "Who?"

"Shiene. The jackrabbit."

"Oh, God. He's not my boyfriend." Carmel laughed shakily. "Look, he's not. I promise."

"Bret said he saw you making out with him. Getting groped."

"Who's Bret?"

"Uh." Sierra's tail tip curled in on itself. "Never mind that. Were you?"

Carmel looked across the lounge, where people were starting to filter up from the lobby. "Yeah, maybe. Look, I can't really get into it."

"Why not?" Sierra lowered his voice. "Sorry. Why not? What's the harm?"

"Never tell someone your plan—"

"—unless they need to know it. Right, I know. But Carm, this is me. You brought me in on a million-dollar deal without so much as telling me what the fuck I was buying. So what's different about this?"

The coyote's eyes shifted. "You might take it into your head to do something."

"I promise, I won't."

Carmel patted him on the arm. "I know you won't. And the way I know is that I won't tell you."

In fifteen years, Sierra had developed a lot of experience in reading people. He'd learned from watching Carmel himself, and had taken that knowledge and built on it. He had made games for himself where he would bet what people would say when he said a particular phrase, and had gotten very good at them. And he stared into the coyote's eyes and had no idea what Carmel was thinking.

"Christ, Carm," he said.

"I know I don't have any right to ask you this, but please—" the coyote said.

"Don't say, 'trust me.'"

The large triangular ears flattened. "All right, then, I won't. But will you?"

"No."

Carmel sighed. The background noise of the lounge grew louder; a couple sat at the table next to them. Sierra sat still, stubbornly refusing to look away or speak again. "Well," Carmel said finally, "I'll see you tomorrow night, then."

His paw brushed Sierra's as he stood. Sierra didn't say anything as the coyote walked away, threading his way easily through the tables so deftly that the people sitting never looked up, barely reacted with more than a flick of the ear, a twitch of the whisker, as he passed.

Sierra tapped the table. If Carmel was worried that Sierra would do something if he told him, then probably it was because Sierra would do something. And that meant that the snow leopard wanted to do something.

He didn't know what he would do, but he had a pretty good idea of where he would do it.

1997: PROMISES

After the concert, Sierra and Carmel talked less and didn't see each other outside of class for a week. Sierra made excuses not to go to the computer lab or to the café—dance practice with Natasha, dinner with his strict host family, and once because Natasha had insisted he meet her parents, an excruciating evening during which Sierra had to dance around the real reasons his parents were on a military base a thousand miles away, and he was here.

Whenever he thought about fulfilling his promise to Carmel, he pictured his clothes coming off only to have police sirens sound and lights come through the window. Ridiculous, he told himself time and again, but even when he forced himself to not think about police, the thought of taking off his clothes with Carmel stirred vague discomfort. He didn't want to talk to Carmel about it, so he just avoided the coyote.

Sierra hadn't thought there was anything wrong, that Carmel was giving him time to recover and work things out. And then he saw the coyote walking around with a handsome fox he didn't recognize, one who wasn't from school.

He'd tried to corner Carmel and ask about the fox, but now it was the coyote's turn to avoid him. He left class a moment early, hurried through the hallways, and was gone almost before the clock ticked up to four o'clock. Sierra made some vague noises to Natasha about meeting her the next day, and walked through the city telling himself that Carmel was just walking around—walking closely, tails brushing—with another friend—a handsome friend, whose shirt opened to reveal his chest ruff— and that there was nothing unusual about it.

Then he sat in the patio outside the café and Carmel walked up to the street corner with the fox, and the two of them held paws, their noses almost touching. Carmel reached up to ruffle the exposed chest ruff, and the fox walked away.

Sierra recognized the fox then: one of the foxes who groomed trails at the Tartok Resort. He'd seen him on the slopes, snowsuit open at the chest as if he didn't really care that much about the cold, and it had only taken Sierra this long to recognize him because he wasn't wearing the ski goggles. But this afternoon, he must have come right from the mountain, and he was wearing that same snowsuit, and it was open at the chest just like his shirt had been that morning.

"So," Sierra said as the coyote came up to him, "done with your friend?"

"Oh, heh." Carmel turned. The fox's ears were still visible above the crowd. "You saw him."

"Of course I saw him."

"Well," the coyote said, "I'm waiting while you do all the stuff you need to do for the dance, for Natasha."

The two of them stood amidst the tables on the patio. Some of the other patrons looked up curiously. Sierra flicked his tail tip. "You didn't say anything about him."

Carmel shrugged. "Would you have wanted me to tell you about him before I did it?"

"Did you think I wouldn't find out?"

The coyote's ears slid back. "I didn't really care if you found out. If you'd asked me I would've told you."

Two badgers were openly watching them now. Sensibilities over here were different; people had arguments in the open and it was okay to watch. Sierra had grown up in the more private culture of the States, and it weirded him out when people had loud discussions in public, and now here he was doing it. "Let's go inside," he said.

"I don't even know why you're upset," Carmel said behind the snow leopard. Sierra's tail lashed back and forth, brushing Carmel's legs.

"Really," Sierra said without turning around. "You don't know."

He found an empty table against the wall, a little round wooden table with a narrow vase holding a flower, and slammed himself down into the creaking wooden chair on the left. Carmel pulled out the chair on the right and sat carefully, letting his tail hang out to one side. "I don't," he repeated. "We never said we wouldn't see other people. You're spending all your time with Natasha, anyway."

"That's—" Sierra lowered his voice. "That's different."

"Why?" Carmel asked it innocently, eyes wide.

"Because you know I'm not doing anything with her. Not until after the dance."

"You made out with her," Carmel pointed out. "In the rain."

Sierra shifted in his chair. "That was—that wasn't—I mean, that's not the point."

"So what is the point?"

Sierra stared at the coyote, at the glossy black nose and tan-furred muzzle, at the forward-perked triangular ears and the ragged cheek ruffs, at the paws clasped beneath the chin and the splayed whiskers, and most of all at the brown eyes. "The point is…" He cleared his throat. "The point is…" Anger was giving way to hurt, and the conversation wasn't any easier here than it would have been at the concert. "The point…"

"You don't want me spending time with him," Carmel said, gently.

"Well…" The snow leopard shifted in his seat, and felt the chair wobble beneath him. "I mean, I am spending time with Natasha. It's just that…"

"Maybe I'd prefer you don't spend so much time with Natasha." The coyote's expression didn't change, and he said the words very off-handedly, as though he were suggesting Sierra get a cappuccino rather than an espresso.

Sierra frowned. "You know I have to. I told her I would."

"You told her. So tell her you've changed your mind."

He said it so casually that Sierra had to shake his head. "I can't. I made her a promise."

"Do you love her?"

Sierra curled his tail around the legs of his chair and shifted his weight again. "It doesn't matter."

Carmel leaned forward. "All I'm saying is, if your feelings have changed, then you should tell her. Don't just go through with the dance for an awkward night of touching a girl's boobs."

"That's not—is that all you think this is about?" Sierra's heart raced. He looked around to see if anyone had heard.

"Isn't it?" Now Carmel inclined his head. "Is there more?"

"Well, sure. I mean, Natasha's sweet. She's nice." At Carmel's expression, Sierra folded his arms. "She is. When you get to know her. I mean, she's straightforward. She doesn't like that she has to do all this stuff, but she realizes that she has to. And she's willing to do what she can to make it worth my while."

"I'm not doubting that. Well, some of it. I think you're seeing what you want to see. But you know, the thing is, I'm willing to wait, but I got to talking to Trevor there, and…" He spread his paws. "Maybe we should talk about this? You want me to promise I won't go out with anyone until you're ready?"

"N-no." When he put it like that, it didn't seem fair at all.

"You want me to not take anyone else to one of the lodges?"

Sierra unfolded his arms. His ears flattened. "You took him to the lodge?" The words caught in his chest, and he struggled to pull in a breath.

The coyote smiled and reached across the table. He tapped Sierra's paw with his fingers. "No, dear. I didn't take him to the lodge. Would you prefer I didn't?"

"Yeah. I guess I would prefer that." Sierra took in a breath and held it. Carmel withdrew his fingers, and Sierra exhaled, slowly. "I'm sorry," he said. "This is really confusing."

"It's not that confusing." Carmel grinned. "You want to be with me, but you think you should be with her."

"I kinda want to be with her, too, though."

The coyote nodded. "Well, so you're attracted to guys and girls. But if it were a choice between me and her, who would you pick?"

Heart and head sparred briefly. Natasha was the obvious answer, and she was nice enough that he had been able to tell himself for weeks that even if they wouldn't keep dating after Tartok, even if there wouldn't be a family, at least it would get him through. His mother had loved the picture of the two of them from the ski lodge, and he could just tell them they'd broken up at the end of school. That would be the end of it, and he would graduate having fulfilled all of his parents' expectations.

And at the heart of it, maybe that was what had cooled him toward Natasha. He was behaving because he was afraid of getting caught. He was afraid of being banned from the military career his father wanted, depriving his mother of the grandcubs she wanted, of living alone without the family he had been brought up to expect. Besides, he did like girls, he really did. He had bookmarked a dozen porn sites that proved it.

But he'd been thinking about Carmel in the shower, as much as he'd been thinking about Natasha. And if Natasha had gone off with some fox from the ski slopes…Sierra turned that possibility over in his mind. Would he have been as upset?

"Look," he said. "Just give me until after the dance. Then I won't see her anymore."

Carmel grinned. His ears perked straight up and his tail swished back and forth through the air. At the time, Sierra thought he knew what that meant. Later, he would not be so sure.

"You sure?"

"No," Sierra said, "but I don't care."

He was in the lodge with Natasha the next day, one arm around her shoulder as she rested into the curve of his chest, when he saw the fox—Trevor—walk into the bar with a bat on his arm. Sierra was a little surprised that they were so obviously together, that Trevor was nuzzling the guy's face, almost kissing him right there in public, until the bat walked off and Sierra saw the slight breasts that her wings had hidden.

He watched the fox a little more closely. Trevor's long, bushy tail, immaculately groomed, swung behind him lazily as he leaned on the bar. Above the tail, the tight jeans showed off his trim, muscular rear. Sierra watched the white tip move back and forth, like a pendulum, and his own tail twitched in response.

"Excuse me," he said to Natasha. "You want another drink?"

"Oh." She tipped her glass to her muzzle and handed it to him, leaning forward for a short kiss. "Sure. Thanks, sweetheart."

Trevor took no notice of Sierra as the snow leopard came up next to him at the bar. Sierra studied the russet muzzle and the tall black ears, looking just like Carmel's. He supposed he could see what the coyote saw in him. If you liked that sort of thing. He pushed Natasha's glass to the bartender and asked for another vodka gimlet, then turned to Trevor.

"Hey," he said.

The fox grunted in reply. Sierra watched the bartender fill Natasha's glass, and got his change ready to pay. "Hey, um, I'm a friend of Carmel's."

He didn't know what he wanted, only that he wanted to understand what was going on. Maybe apologize if Trevor was hurt that Carmel was leaving him, or somehow get Trevor to admit what he'd done with Carmel. Maybe more that last one.

As it turned out, it was easier than he'd imagined. The fox turned and looked him up and down. "*Il* coyote?"

Sierra nodded. Trevor took a drink of his beer and wiped his muzzle. "*Si*, so, you want the same deal? I give you same price."

"Price?" Sierra flushed. His warm ears flattened. "Uh, how much…"

"Fifteen francs." The fox pointed a finger at him. "Each time. No more of this, one time morning, one time afternoon, all count as one day. Morning, fifteen francs. Afternoon, fifteen francs. *Si?*"

"Oh," Sierra said. "Well, that's a bit more than I thought, just for, uh…well, I mean, maybe I could get less than he got?"

"Less?" Trevor laughed. "So you want Trevor to come down, say hello, go away? Mmmh." He shrugged his shoulders. "Still fifteen francs."

"Wait." The bat exited the bathroom and began to make her way back to the bar, so he talked fast. "Um, what did you do with Carmel? I mean, he only told me about…about…he said you were really good…"

The bat arrived back at the bar. She leaned forward and smiled at Sierra. "Good day," she said, and then, to Trevor, "Friend of yours, Trev?"

"No, he wants the same thing as that *finnochio*-te wanted." Trevor laughed. "You see, is *finnochio* and coyote, so *finnochio*-te…no, he asks if I will come down to school and walk with him. Maybe let him touch my chest." He reached up and fluffed the thick ruff under his chin. "Everybody want to be seen with Trevor."

All they'd done was walk? Sierra stared at the fox's sneer, at the cooing way the bat reached over to touch his chest ruff as well. He didn't know what *finnochio* meant, but from the way the fox said it, he had a pretty good idea.

His mouth was dry. He picked up Natasha's drink. "All you did was walk with him?"

"*Si, si.*" Trevor had already turned toward the bat, though his ear flicked Sierra's way.

"That's funny." Sierra took a sip of Natasha's drink to moisten his tongue. "He said you really liked being buggered."

He stayed long enough to see the bat's muzzle twist, then walked away quickly. When he sat next to Natasha, he looked back at the bar. The bat had stepped back a couple paces, winged arms on her hips, as Trevor pleaded with her. She turned and walked out, and he shot one venomous glance at Sierra before following her.

"What did you say to him?" Natasha said, following his look.

Sierra shrugged. "Just asked him what to do around here when we're not skiing. He offered to walk me around, for a price."

"But you know what we do." Natasha snuggled back into him. "Anyway, I'll walk around with you for free."

"I know," he said, and draped his arm around her shoulder.

2012: END GAME

The problem with hotel rooms was that there wasn't anywhere you could hide and watch the door. Sierra walked up and down the hallway on the second floor of the Pine building, past the Shienes' room, and then down to the lobby of the Pine building. The best place to observe, it turned out, was from an adjacent building, where he could sit by a window with his laptop and watch the grey stone archway with the pine tree etched into the keystone. A guy sitting by a window with a laptop was not creepy. Not as creepy, anyway.

Sunset painted the brick walls with bright fire, which faded to a mottled purple and then eventually the black of night. It was harder to see the people go in and out of the building, but the light over the entrance casting a small pool of light onto the first ten feet of stone pathway helped. Sierra had to just keep his head down over his laptop, and mostly the people who walked by him didn't bother him. One, a hotel employee, asked if he needed anything in his room, and he said he liked the view from this window better.

At about eight-thirty, a jackrabbit left the building, but she was female, in the company of three others. Sierra watched her thoughtfully, and his ears perked. He had assumed that whatever Carmel was doing was okay with the wife; Shiene had been making out with the coyote in the lobby, and he had to know that word would get back to her. But maybe he was one of those guys who just thought he was being discreet without actually understanding how to do that. Maybe he thought that hiding under a staircase was enough to keep his wife from hearing about his torrid gay romance.

The image of the jackrabbit on top of Carmel, thrusting into him, came into Sierra's mind. He squeezed his eyes shut and shook his head to dispel it. It was Carmel's business; he didn't owe Sierra anything. And Sierra would have been happy to leave the coyote to his business, except that he could not, *could not* get rid of the feeling that there was something not quite right about it. All he had to go on was Carmel saying that Sierra would do something if he knew about it, and the only thing Sierra could think to do was to barge in and find out what it was. Maybe stop it, maybe not.

It was frustrating as hell not being able to read the coyote better, like finding a book in a foreign language in a library. Sierra turned back to his laptop. Maybe he was just doing this out of jealousy. He stared down at the code he'd been writing. He should just go back to his room, finish working on this, and wait 'til the next day when Carmel would meet him and tell him what was going on. Trust the coyote.

If only that had worked better in the past.

No. He wasn't going to get involved without knowing the whole scene. He'd already tempted fate once with the skunk, and yeah, he was pretty good at improv, but he hadn't known Carmel was already working something. He could've screwed everything up.

He closed the laptop and sat there with it closed in his lap. Back to the room, shove aside the jealous feelings, and wake up tomorrow. Carmel would be fine.

Then he glanced out the window and saw Carmel and Shiene walking into the building.

The jackrabbit moved with urgency, tall ears alert, paw on the coyote's rear, under his tail. Carmel's ears were flicking about, his muzzle turning in quick darts, more worried than Shiene about whether someone was watching. He turned toward Sierra, and though the hallway behind the snow leopard was dark, it wasn't impossible that Carmel might see a shape there.

Sierra flattened himself against the wall. Carmel's muzzle turned away again without giving any sign that he'd noticed, and he hurried into the building, propelled by the jackrabbit's paw on his butt.

The snow leopard chewed his lip and fingered the plastic card in his pocket. He stared down at the empty entryway again. He realized that all his attempts to talk himself out of doing this had basically been stalling his departure until Carmel showed up, so that he would now have no choice.

You have a choice. You always have a choice.

Two minutes later, he stood under the light, eyes fixed on the stairway beyond the glass doors. Carmel was probably fine, probably just working a scam. A scam that involved…what? And what if this jackrabbit really was a boyfriend? What if the guy was going to leave his wife and run off with Carmel, and Carmel just wouldn't tell Sierra straight up because he never told Sierra anything straight up, because he was trying to string Sierra along again?

He slammed the heel of his paw against the brick next to the door. What had he learned over the last fifteen years, if nothing else? Go and find out for himself. He pushed open the glass door and shook himself, walking from the cold of night into the warm building, and without hesitation, stepped onto the stair.

There was a badger in the upstairs hall just leaving her room, so he walked past her as though going farther along, then turned around when she'd gone and doubled back to Shiene's room. He put his ear to the door, but the hotel doors were thick and soundproof, even to species with sharper ears than his.

The locks weren't silent, which meant that they would hear him as soon as he put the key in the door. Sorry, he practiced in his head. They must have given me the wrong room. So sorry. And he would back away. Carmel was practiced enough to not give away any sign of recognition, and Sierra would apologize after. If anything, Carmel would be impressed that he'd been resourceful enough to get the key.

He took a deep breath and put his ear to the door one more time. Still nothing.

Below his paw, below the white plastic card with the picture of the pine tree on it, the black slot of the lock waited. He looked down at it, and then thrust the card in and pulled it out.

A light blinked green, and the mechanical lock whirred. Sierra slammed the handle down and walked in as though it were his room.

It looked exactly like his room, at least in the details that first caught his eye: the bedspread, the painting on the wall, the balcony window and the desk. But then there were differences: the red bag on the luggage stand, the powerful smell of jackrabbit, the scents of lavender and vanilla from the bathroom. And there was another important difference: the coyote on his back on the bed, legs drawn up to reveal his bare rear, and the jackrabbit kneeling in front of him, glistening erection dangling between his legs as he pressed two fingers into the coyote. Both of them had turned to look at Sierra, and the jackrabbit pulled his fingers out as though he'd been burned.

"What the *fuck?*" the jackrabbit said. He grabbed part of the bedspread and held it up against his leg, probably in the mistaken impression that it was hiding his erection. "Who are you?"

"I'm. Jesus, I'm sorry," Sierra said. "They must have given me the wrong key…"

"Well, this isn't a fucking show. Get the hell out!" Shiene backed off the bed, still holding the bedspread up over his crotch, still not completely hiding himself. He glared at the snow leopard, his eyes blazing with hunger, muzzle open. He was panting, and not, Sierra thought, just with arousal. He had an expression Sierra had seen on his own face, as recently as the last couple days, when something he'd been longing for for years

lay tantalizingly close.

Carmel, too, was looking at Sierra, and he looked honestly surprised, not upset. The snow leopard lingered a moment, pushing aside his own feelings to try to divine what the coyote wanted him to do. He was also finding it difficult to look away from Carmel's tail and rear, which he'd only seen in dreams for the last fifteen years. But the coyote's eyes—when he could force himself to look that way—remained large and brown and fixed on him, and the triangular ears were perfectly still. They weren't back, or flat; they weren't flicking one way or another. The only thing Sierra could think was that he had done something completely unexpected, and Carmel didn't know how to react.

When in doubt…he should just walk out. There'd be no harm done. Shiene didn't know him, and Carmel hadn't given him away yet. He took a step back.

The jackrabbit took a step forward, free paw bunched in a fist, muscles tight and tense in his arm, fur bristling over his shoulders. His erection had withdrawn into his sheath a little, but that was not much consolation to Sierra. It wouldn't take long for them to resume once he left.

He swallowed. "Actually, um." He pointed at Carmel. "That's my boyfriend."

The jackrabbit swiveled his tall ears to Carmel without taking his eyes from Sierra. He narrowed his gaze and set his jaw, but he did relax, his fur settling down. "So?" he said.

Behind him, Carmel was staring at Sierra, and now his ears had gone slightly askew, his eyebrows pinched together with worry. Sierra cleared his throat. The room felt suffocatingly warm. "So, uh…"

"Look," Shiene said, "You work that out on your own time. Right now I got about twenty more minutes and so either back the fuck out or get your clothes off and your tail up and get in line."

"Get in line?" Sierra's whiskers flattened back against his muzzle and his ears lowered.

"No!" Carmel called.

Both of them turned to him. His ears were down, and he looked apologetically at Shiene. "I'll talk to Kotrat later. Hon, why don't you go back to the room and wait there. I'm sorry I didn't tell you more about what was going on, but we've talked about this, you know? Just give me a little time to spend with Cory here. This is the only chance he has to get away from his wife."

"And I have to Neutra-Scent the room after," Shiene growled. "I've been waiting all fucking week for this, so get lost." He hitched up the bedspread, more successfully hiding the imminent coitus from Sierra's eyes. "If I don't hear that door close in two seconds, I swear to God I'll throw you off that balcony."

His ears folded down, a deliberate dismissal. He might not really be able to go through with it in front of an audience, but he wanted Sierra to think he would. The snow leopard swallowed and met Carmel's eyes one more time. The coyote's ears flicked to either side, and then up. *Go.*

In three steps, he was out of the room, the door swinging shut behind him. Carmel had been trying to tell him something. He paced quickly down the hall, down the stairs and out of the stifling heat into the crisp, cold air.

A mash of footprints in the snow led away from the building, most of them along the path to the main lodge. *Be patient*, Carmel had said. *This is the only time he can get away from his wife.*

And then he saw the female jackrabbit coming toward him, striding purposefully across the path, and he understood.

She brushed past him and into the building, ears up, jaw tight. She hadn't bothered to put on a coat over the long orange dress she wore, and up close she was really quite lovely. A pair of pearls dotted the tips of her ears, matching the ones in the gold necklace that sparkled in her creamy yellow throat fur, and the curve of her dress as she went up the stairs was, if not a fashion magazine ideal, certainly flattering enough.

Sierra walked up the stairs, but the only trace of her presence was a whiff of vanilla scent and the soft brushing of her paws on the carpet in a purposeful rhythm. He crept to the corner without going around and waited there.

A door opened. "Cory!" a female voice shouted. "Oh my God!"

The door slammed again. Sierra, taken aback, had just enough presence of mind to run down the stairs as feet thudded along the hallway behind him. He got to the door and turned in time to see the jackrabbit—Mrs. Shiene, he presumed—stride purposefully down the stairs.

Her expression was not shocked, nor distraught. Rather, she looked like someone who had experienced a hunger like Sierra's or her husband's, and had just had it sated.

1997: ENDGAME

Sierra sat out in front of the café, fingers curled around a warm mug, and didn't look up when Carmel sat down. "Espresso," the coyote told the waiter, and then he leaned forward. "You okay? You were awful quiet in school today."

"I'm fine." Sierra exhaled. The air was warm enough that he couldn't see his breath.

The coyote tilted his head and cupped both ears forward. "You sure?"

"What's it to you, anyway?"

Carmel's brown paw slid across the table and rested fingers on Sierra's wrist. "Where did that come from?"

The snow leopard shrugged. "Came from me."

"Okay." Carmel breathed out. Sierra smelled meat faintly below the spearmint flavor of Carmel's mints. "So what'd I do? Is this about Trevor? I thought we were okay with that."

"We were," Sierra said. "Or, we would have been. If you'd been telling me the truth about him."

"I didn't tell you anything about him."

Sierra looked up at the coyote. Mischief danced in the brown eyes, though his expression remained serious. "You just saw me with him, you drew conclusions, and we talked about whether we were seeing other people."

"Then you let me believe a lie."

Carmel shook his head. "I didn't work you, if that's what you think."

"How did you not work me?" Sierra raised his voice. "You paid a guy to walk around with you and look like you were dating him."

"Okay." Carmel grinned. "So what does that say about how I feel about you?"

"I guess it's flattering." Sierra shook his head. "Why couldn't you just tell me? Talk to me about it?"

"We did talk."

"After you set all that up. After you put on that show."

Carmel shrugged. "I thought a demonstration would be more effective. If you're just thinking about things and trying to weigh them back and forth, well…you know, it's all abstract. It doesn't really affect your life. I thought maybe you would be okay with me seeing someone else and then it wouldn't be a big deal. But you weren't. So it got you thinking about what you wanted."

"It seems like a lot of trouble to go through."

"I saw it on The Young and the Restless. It worked then, too."

Sierra raised his eyebrows. "You watch soap operas?"

"We get TV from the States, and my mom likes them. We sort of watch them together."

"Jesus, I miss TV from home." Sierra sighed and rubbed the side of his muzzle. "Are we in a soap opera? Is that what's going on? Because I feel like that sometimes."

The waiter brought Carmel's espresso and left with a flick of his ringed tail. Carmel ignored the tiny cup and the strong rich smell. "Do you have an evil twin? Because that might actually help. He could go to the dance with Natasha while you spend the night with me."

"Yeah, but he'd be evil. So he'd probably ditch Natasha and trick me into doing something else so he could have you all to himself." He smiled.

Carmel laughed. "So are you still going to the dance?"

"Well, yeah. I have to."

Carmel shook his head. "I keep telling you, you make your own future. You don't have to go with her."

"But I can't let her down."

The coyote picked up his espresso and blew gently on it. "It's let her down now, or let her down later, right?"

"No, she's—she knows we won't keep going out after the dance. It's just something nice I should do for her."

"The thing is," Carmel said, "my parents are going out of town the weekend of the dance. There's a special event up in Bruxe and they're leaving Friday noon, back on Sunday."

"So we can go to your place Saturday night."

The coyote shook his head. "Our housekeeper will be there the whole time, and I'm not allowed to have guests. There's secure stuff in Dad's study." He rolled his eyes. "Like you would care. But the housekeeper won't let anyone but me in. But…" his eyes gleamed. "I know where the car keys are kept."

"They're not driving?"

"No, it's an embassy thing, and they're flying."

Sierra rubbed his fingers along the ceramic of his mug. The coffee in it was cooling, and he hadn't had very much of it. "Where did you have in mind?"

Carmel's smile broadened. "There's a hotel in Lutèce—"

"Lutèce!" Sierra let go of the mug. "Why not a local hotel?"

"Why not the lodge?"

Sierra narrowed his eyes. "You mean the lodge where Princess Kelly stayed? Or the ones that were just built seven years ago and made to look old and rustic?"

"Oh." Carmel flicked his ears. "It was a nice story, right?"

"Have you told me the truth about anything?"

Carmel raised his eyebrows. "Why did you get in trouble at your last school?"

"Jesus." Sierra stared down at his coffee.

"Make something up, if you don't want to tell me."

Sierra took a breath. "I was in high school near Millenport. And I played around with computers a lot. You know, Dad got reassigned every couple years. All my friends were on the computer, and one of them started doing this hacker challenge."

"Oh." Carmel leaned forward, ears cupped. "And you were good at it."

"Good enough." He closed his eyes and could still see the green text on black, the terminal shell that had let him into so many closed doors, the alien environment that he'd learned to feel at home in, that he'd been banned from. "So my friend got the idea that, you know, there was this big government building just up the road, and he bet me I couldn't get us into that."

"Big government..." Carmel's brow creased. "You mean the Center for Biological—you broke into the CBD?"

"We didn't get far," Sierra said. "I cracked the gate entry code and had authorization, but it was just the two of us, dumb kids, and the guard stopped us at the gate." And called his father, and made them wait three hours for his father to come pick them up, with Rey's father, who drove their car back. The two of them, separated in silent cars for an hour. He hadn't spoken more than four words to Rey since then.

"I think you were a very smart kid," Carmel said. "I can't believe we've been wasting our time cadging pastries."

Sierra shook his head. "I don't do that anymore."

"Whoever that other kid was, he's a mook," Carmel said. "You deserve a real partner."

The words hit Sierra harder than he'd expected. He tensed and forced emotion back down his throat, shook his head more violently. "Come on," Carmel said. "You broke into a highly secure government facility when you were seventeen!"

"I was…" Wrong, stupid, reckless, disobedient, wilful, wasting his life. "Young."

"You're older now." Carmel smiled. "Is that a true story?"

Sierra raised his head and looked the coyote in the eyes, and just raised his eyebrows. Carmel laughed. "Fair enough. Look, I'm sorry about the stories. Come with me this weekend and I promise, no more stories. I'll be honest with you." He put a paw over his heart and widened his eyes. "Scout's honor."

"You, a scout?" Sierra snorted, but the emotion was subsiding, and he smiled because he felt like smiling. "If we go…why not just one of the hotels around here?"

"There's a little club in Lutèce I want to go to. It's open 'til 2 am so there'd be plenty of time to get there if we leave at four or five."

"We could take the train."

Carmel raised his eyebrows. "The two of us traveling together on a train?"

"The foxes took the train up last month."

The coyote sipped his espresso and drummed his fingers on the tabletop. "They're used to it. I like the freedom of driving. My parents drove me to Lutèce a couple times. We stopped for dinner at this cute little town, a really nice restaurant. The *coq au vin* was amazing. You want to eat dinner on the train?"

"I hate to keep pointing out problems," Sierra said, "but the restaurant and the hotel all sound sort of expensive. Are we going to work them?"

"Do you want to do this?"

The pull of Carmel and the adventure battered at his defenses. He made one last-ditch effort to save a night with Natasha and, better still, the freedom from obligation to her. "What if we went to the club Saturday night and left first thing in the morning? We could get back by noon."

"You really want to go to the dance."

Sierra shifted in his seat, tail curling around his legs. "I promised."

"So you want to go to the dance and then sleep with her, and then get in the car with me for six hours, and come and sleep with me."

Carmel wasn't making much effort to lower his voice. A red panda at the next table perked an ear and looked quickly at them. Sierra whispered, "I don't—I don't have to sleep with her. I guess."

"That'll be better. So you'll go to the dance and then say, 'Sorry, I don't really want to sleep with you.' That's sure to go over well."

Oh God, she would kill him. "I'll clean up, I guess," he tried to say, and then even though he felt Carmel was about to acquiesce, he said, "No. That's not fair to you. I'll—I'll just tell her I can't go."

"Tell her you got sick." Carmel did lower his voice for that. "Don't go to school Friday."

"My host family—"

"Leave as if you're going to school. Call in the afternoon and tell them you're staying with me for the weekend. I'll come over."

"But you can't have visitors—oh. They don't know that."

Carmel reached a paw across the table. "I'll go to school and tell them I'm picking up your assignments for you. And I'll tell Natasha the bad news. She might call you. You hang out at the park. When school's out, I'll come get you, we'll drive up to Lutèce, we'll drive back Saturday, I'll drop you at your host family's place."

"What if Natasha comes over and asks about my fever?"

The coyote shrugged. "Has she ever come to your house before?"

"Well…" He hesitated. "No."

"All right." Teeth showed in a long grin. "Up for some adventure, then?"

Sierra inhaled. The smells of coffee and coyote mixed in his nose on the warm spring air. Going to the dance with Natasha would be safe, would be playing by the rules. He grinned. "Yeah. Let's do it."

Carmel squeezed his paw, and Sierra squeezed back. "Now, about the money," the coyote said, leaning closer. "Get it from your parents. Say you need to take out your girl for the dance."

"They'll find out after…"

"After is after. You've been pretty good all year, right? You'll get a summer job, you'll pay them back. Or we can work some tourists here, make it back over the summer."

The coyote's easy confidence was catching. Sierra could see any number of things that could go wrong—what if the car broke down? What if Natasha and his host family and Carmel's housekeeper all talked to each other? What if, what if, what if—but the more he thought about the risk, the faster his heart beat. A smile curved at the edges of his mouth. He was close to graduation, and what could his parents do after that? He was the one who was going to determine the track of his life, and he'd be damned if he was just going to keep going round and round on their path. He could show Carmel he was just as good at adventures as the coyote was.

He met Carmel's sparkling eyes and knew that whatever might go wrong, whatever would happen to the two of them, they would be in it together.

2012: STORIES

He had only been sitting at the desk in his room for five minutes, staring at the painting of a lake surrounded by wildflowers, when the knock came, almost lost in the Valhalla song he'd called up on his computer. He said, "Come in," without getting up, because he'd flipped the sliding bolt and let the door close on it. Carmel pushed the door open and stood in the hallway, hesitating.

The coyote had dressed hastily, his jeans still hanging open a little at the front and his shirt only partly buttoned, and he carried something bunched in his paw that might be an undershirt, or underwear. The dark tip of his tail was just visible against his jeans, at the knee where it curled around his leg. His ears were down but not completely flat, and over his shoulder he carried a messenger bag.

"Er…" Carmel glanced around the room before his gaze settled on Sierra. "Can I use your shower?"

"Sure." Sierra nodded toward the door. "Lock that, would you?"

"Course." The coyote flipped the sliding bolt back, let the door swing shut, and closed the bolt again over it. The music wailed, "*Someday I'll fly away/Escape this wheel and rise up high.*"

"You can come in," Sierra said when Carmel didn't move from the hallway. "You're freaking me out a bit."

"That's Valhalla, right?"

Sierra nodded, just as Joey Stone screamed, "*Rise up hiiiiiiigh,*" and the song ended. He shut off his music player.

"Sorry about the lead singer. At least you got to meet him."

"Yeah. Guess that was the only way out he could figure out."

Carmel sighed. "Do you want the explanation before or after the shower?" The coyote took a step forward and dropped the clothes he was holding to the floor. The bundle unfolded into a shirt and a pair of underpants.

"After's fine. Do you have any other clothes?"

"In a locker at the rental place." The coyote grinned and dropped the messenger bag onto the floor. It landed with a laptop-heavy thud.

"You just scammed a guy—I'm assuming—out of a million dollars, and you're living out of a locker?"

"I thought you wanted the explanation after the shower."

Sierra waved him to the bathroom and turned back to his laptop, but even though there was activity on the hacker forums, he barely registered it as he scrolled past. It felt like a dream, that he was here in a hotel with Carmel Coyote again, that after all these years he was going to get answers.

He shut the laptop and paced up and down in the room, listening to the sound of water, the breaks in the flow as Carmel scrubbed his fur. He wanted to run in there with him; he wanted to go to the door and yell at him to hurry up. Neither of those would help. He forced himself to sit on the foot of the bed with his knees drawn up, trying not to think about Lutèce, the good and the bad of it, and failing.

The elaborate four-poster bed so close to the antique dresser that they had to turn sideways to walk between. The smell of age noticeable over the Neutra-Scent, the accumulation of years in the wood around the window, the ceiling plaster, the corners. All the signage in French, Sierra noticing but too keyed up to try out his year of study on it. His paws sinking into the carpet in quick steps, and then his rear sinking down into the bed. "Wow."

"Feathers." Carmel looking down, his knees touching Sierra's, only a breath away, his scent crowding out everything else: confident, strong coyote scent.

The lights of Lutece sparkling through the window. Sierra's heart pounding. Carmel gently placing both paws on his cheeks. The touch of lips, the darkness as his eyes close, Sierra sinking into the moment.

Forever later, the coyote pulling his muzzle back, paws staying where they are. "Hi."

"Hi." Sierra's smile stretching wide. Licking his lips just a little.

"You want to grab food first?"

Sierra's paws trembling at the clasp of his belt. "I…I want to grab you first."

Carmel kissing him again, then taking one step back, which pressed him against the wall. Carmel unbuttoning his shirt, letting it fall open to show his chest. Reaching for the clasp of his pants as Sierra pushed his own down.

The bathroom door opened, releasing the powerful scent of shampoo and wet coyote. Carmel rummaged in the closet and then stepped out into the main bedroom area, fastening a white bathrobe around his waist.

"You haven't used your robes," he said. He climbed onto the bed and sat cross-legged, looking diagonally across the bedspread at Sierra.

The snow leopard turned to face the coyote, staying seated. "Never had company here I didn't mind being naked in front of."

"The pine marten at the desk?"

Sierra blinked back his surprise. "Yeah. Couple times, actually."

The coyote raised an eyebrow. "I can smell him. I mean, given what you just saw me doing, it's not a big deal."

"I'd hope not." Sierra didn't smile, didn't betray the little flutter in his heart that Carmel might be jealous of Bret. "So you were planning on getting caught by the guy's wife. Someone hired you to get him in trouble?"

"She hired me." Carmel folded his paws in the white cloth over his lap. "Guys like to mess around on their wives, and the wives don't really care, except when the guys are real assholes about it. So the wife catches him *in flagrante coyote*, he apologizes and gets her a Lexus or a diamond or a trip to Playa or whatever."

"And you get?"

The coyote spread his paws. "Depends on the case. Ten thou, twenty. That one was fifteen."

"Can't she just buy herself a trip to Playa for fifteen thou?"

"Well, it also keeps the husband more faithful to her, at least for a couple years. If she just wanted money, she'd divorce him." Carmel's ears perked up and he smiled. "There's still some love there. That's why I do it."

"That buys a lot of bus lockers."

"I don't keep most of the money. Just enough to live on 'til the next conference."

Sierra blinked. "Here I was imagining you had a big estate out in the country, or over…like you used to talk about. You give away a million every time?"

"Nah. Usually couple hundred thou. This was a big one, though. Been chasing that guy for five years, setting up my references so he'd trust me, getting my name in some financial papers. Whiz kid, that's me." He grinned and held up a paw, wiggling his fingers, but the grin faded when Sierra didn't answer it, and he dropped his paw.

"So who gets the money?"

"Green World. Pro-environment action group. The senior director there is a background partner. He puts all the right stuff out on the website, and then in about two weeks he'll announce that the endorsement that was going to make millions for my fictional company is being reversed."

"Endorsement?"

"Green World has government and industry ties, and the companies they endorse often get big industry contacts. My partner there has lots of connections all over." Carmel waved a paw. "I can get into some detail, if you want, but not all of it."

Sierra shook his head. "Your 'partner'?"

"Business only."

The snow leopard drew in a breath. Carmel waited patiently.

"Yeah, I want to." Sierra leaning in, insistent.

Carmel's paw caressing his achingly hard shaft. "Have you been practicing?"

"Uh. Some? I don't care. I want to." Reaching out, taking the coyote's similarly hard erection in his paw, smiling when Carmel inhaled sharply. "You're not that big. Not shampoo bottle big."

"Okay." Carmel fake-measuring Sierra's erection between finger and thumb. "The first thing about dating a guy is you never say 'you're not that big.'"

Sierra laughing, Carmel reaching for a small tube. The coyote talking as his fingers rubbed delicately beneath Sierra's tail, the chilly lubricant warming slowly.

The first time, warmth and hardness sliding into him, pain flaring and then ebbing. Carmel asking, "Are you okay, Si?" body tense behind Sierra's.

"I'm good." Sierra closing his eyes. Thinking that 'good' could mean 'terrified and a little sore and excited beyond belief and standing on the precipice of a new life, ready to rise up,' at least in this case. Rise up and leave you all behind, *him and Carmel soaring away. Partners, that was the word for it. So fitting.*

"Do you have a…non-business partner?"

Carmel shook his head slowly. "Dated here and there." He hesitated, then said, "You?"

In the silence, Sierra could hear the whirr of the room's temperature and scent controls. He rested his chin on his knees. "When you're not running a long con, what do you do?"

"That's about all I do. But officially I'm a Green World employee. I do research, interviews. Reporting type stuff, but slanted to our view. Telling stories."

"Saving the world."

"'From the ground up.' That's our slogan."

Sierra's eyebrows rose. "You founded the company?"

"I wrote the slogan." Carmel smiled, and the smile remained even against the pressure of Sierra's silence. "Can I ask you some questions?"

Sierra nodded. Curled around his legs, his tail tip twitched.

Carmel reached up to scratch behind one ear. The wet coyote scent came a little more strongly to Sierra. "Why did you quit your job?"

For a moment, Sierra thought he'd misheard. He slipped into his practiced reaction to surprise: neutral expression, act like you were expecting the question. "A lot of things fell apart at the same time. I decided to start over."

"I saw you sold everything. Almost."

"How long have you been stalking me?"

Carmel's ears flattened. "Just the last five, six years. You're pretty careful with social media, but if you interact with anyone, it leaves traces of you. If you want people to buy most of your worldly possessions, you have to get the word out."

"So you don't interact with anyone."

"Not as 'Carmel.' Not with anyone you'd be able to trace me back through."

"You haven't talked to your parents in years."

The coyote closed his eyes. "Yeah, well. We had a fight. Kind of a big one."

Sierra nodded. "I guessed. They wouldn't say what it was about."

"Terrorism. Sort of. They supported some things that I felt strongly should not be supported. Civil rights violations, that sort of thing. Plus they kind of knew about some of my…extracurriculars. So yeah. We left it there about…nine years ago?" He leaned back against the pillows. "But they talk to you now?"

"Some." Sierra rested a paw on his tail. "I guess it was after your fight, your dad reached out to me. Said he was sorry, that he realized that probably you were the one who got me in trouble, not the other way around."

"How are your parents?"

"Dad's two years from retirement. Mom's joined the VA and campaigned to get 'Don't Ask Don't Tell' repealed. She crusades for gay rights now."

"Cool."

"And your parents are fine too."

Carmel looked away from him, out at the dark window and the

mountain beyond. Again, the pressure of the silence weighed in on Sierra, until it pushed free the question that was choking him. "Carm, what the hell happened in Lutèce?"

Carmel closed his eyes again and swallowed. "Do you hate me?"

"I did, for a while. No, that's a lie. I was just…I was scared and confused and hurt. I felt betrayed."

"That's fair. I did betray you." Carmel opened his eyes and looked right at Sierra. "I…god, I've rehearsed this a million times. I never figured out a way to say it right."

Sierra's ears cupped forward. His paws squeezed each other, freeing his tail, which twitched crazily. He felt a thrill of anticipation, a desperate hope warring with fear of what the coyote would say.

"I fucked it up. I fucked it all up. I swear, I just went out to get coffee and pastries. I swear it. And I came back and I saw the police car, and I just panicked. I ran to the corner and sat in the park for fifteen minutes. Then I thought of you and I ran back, but they were leading you out the door, and…" His fangs showed as he bit the edge of his lip. "I didn't go up there. I thought—I thought that if I could stay free, I could figure out some way to…"

His words trailed off. Sierra's claws were extended, pricking his skin through his fur. "No," Carmel said. "I was afraid to be arrested. That's the truth."

"You could've told them it was your parents' car." Sierra couldn't keep the words in. "You could've explained the diplomat plates, the whole thing."

"I didn't tell you—it was an embassy car. I—then, I was terrified they'd arrest me, too, and my parents would get in trouble." He took a breath. "I figured you were already arrested, and I couldn't help you. By the time I changed my mind about that, it was too late. They wouldn't tell me where you'd gone. I took a train back to Ginebra and I told my parents the truth, I swear I did, but then they asked why you were arrested and I wasn't, and I…" He bit down again before continuing. "I was too ashamed to tell them I ran out on you."

Carmel padding around the bed in the morning. Sierra looking up muzzily, a little sore but relishing the soreness as a badge of initiation, a secret shared between the two of them. "I'll come with."

"Nah." Carmel grinning. "I'm dressed already. I want to eat pastries off your naked stomach. Then lick the crumbs up."

"Mmm. Okay." Sierra stretching and rolling onto his back as the door

closed. That was the kind of joke they would have, the two of them. Licking up crumbs. 'You're not so big.' ON RUM. Feeling not just pleasure, but relief that he'd enjoyed the sex as much as he had. Natasha as a faint glimmer, a road not taken, already behind him.

Fierce joy, feeling as though he'd sprouted wings and taken his first flight. Imagining his parents cutting him off, not caring; images of him and Carmel working games for food, him studying up on his computer skills, Carmel charming his way into jobs, easily making the little they'd need to get by. New life, new Sierra.

The screech of cars out front, the flicker of worry, quickly quenched. Planning what he would say when Carmel returned.

The knock at the door.

"And you didn't try to find me."

"It was too late. I figured you hated me, maybe even thought I called the police on you as a joke."

"That crossed my mind," Sierra said. He took a breath, his eyes sliding away from Carmel. "I thought it was a game, that you'd been playing me. When you got what you wanted…"

"I was playing a game," Carmel said softly. "You figured it out. You called me on it."

"And then it was over!"

Carmel shook his head slowly. "I was playing a game to get you away from…that female snow leopard, whatever her name was."

"Natasha."

The one day he had to say good-bye before being sent to his parents at the military base. The ski lodge, Natasha drinking with Marianne and Gino, her arm around Carlo. Their silence when he walked up. Her pointed refusal to meet his eyes as she said that Carmel had told them everything.

Her laughter when Trevor sucker-punched him in the gut on his way out. Staggering, bent over, toward the exit.

The months of prison-like confinement that summer with his parents, no computer, no phone. The relief and giddy anticipation when he was allowed to check his mail, look at their History of Ginebra website. The lack of messages, of any changes at all. The sensation of betrayal all over again, of falling, and falling, and never reaching bottom.

"She was playing a game, too. She was trying to keep you away from

me."

"But you won the game, and then I wasn't interesting. That's what I thought. She told me you bragged about it."

"I—that bitch. I asked if she'd heard from you, that's all. Maybe I let slip a little about what happened. I was kinda messed up. But I swear I didn't call the police." Carmel raised a paw. "By Lion Christ or Jesus Wolf or Baal or Richard Dawkins, whatever god you want me to swear by."

"How do I know?" Sierra raised his voice. "How do I know this isn't just another story?"

The coyote tilted his head to one side. "Because it's not a very good one, is it? I don't come off very well. I'm sure it's not what you want to hear."

"You never tried to reach me. All those years. You hid from me."

"You didn't try to contact me," Carmel said. "You erased our whole history website. I thought you hated me."

"I was practically in solitary confinement on a military base with my parents!"

"Shit." Carmel's eyes widened. "God, I'm sorry. When I thought about what I did…I wanted to erase that old self of mine, leave it behind."

"So did I." Sierra sighed and stared down at the bedspread. "I don't think you did, though."

"Did what? Want to?"

The snow leopard shook his head. "I don't think you left it behind. This giving away all your money, cutting ties with your parents, getting guys in trouble for being attracted to you…sounds like you're depriving yourself as self-inflicted punishment for something you feel you did wrong."

Carmel shifted his weight on the bed. Sierra saw the coyote's shadow slide forward, ears perked. "Really?"

"Yeah, well. That's what my therapist says."

The silence that followed that statement was not oppressive, but static, as if time had frozen. Sierra felt he could sit staring at the bedspread for hours, days even, and when he looked up it would still be night, and Carmel would still be on the bed, and time would not start again until one of them spoke. The stasis felt comfortable to him, weightless and empty.

Carmel started the clocks. "Si? Can I ask you something?"

"Sure." Sierra kept his head down.

Softly, Carmel said, "Can I hug you?"

Can you? Sierra wanted to ask. *I don't know.* The gulf between them was fifteen years and an ocean wide; it seemed impossible that the coyote's arms could reach that far. But the stasis was cold, even through Sierra's thick fur, and Carmel was right here in the room with him. He nodded, a quick jerk of his head.

The bed shifted as Carmel crawled over to him. The coyote hesitated, then leaned awkwardly over Sierra's knees and tried to circle his neck.

Sierra sighed and dropped his legs to one side, stretching them out on the bed. Carmel straddled them and pressed himself close to Sierra's chest. Wet coyote filled Sierra's nostrils as he lifted his arms, encircling the coyote's body in return.

"I'm sorry, Si," Carmel said. "I'm so sorry."

Sierra held him more tightly, and Carmel squeezed back, and then they were pressed together so closely, muzzles next to each other, fur ruffling with each other's breaths. Carmel panted and rubbed a paw down Sierra's back, and Sierra just held the coyote.

"I'm sorry, too," he whispered.

Carmel pressed his muzzle against the snow leopard's. "For what? You didn't do anything."

To say that he felt as though he'd deserved the betrayal, thought it payback for betraying Natasha, would only make Carmel feel worse. He was doing his best to put those feelings aside, and there was no need to air them now, not yet, perhaps not ever. But there was something he could apologize for without bringing those feelings into it. "I didn't trust you. When you didn't send me any message, I thought…I thought the whole thing was a joke, a game. I thought you'd tricked me into going up there just to abandon me, that you'd called the police to get me in trouble, that all that stuff you'd said wasn't true."

"You had good reason."

"No." He rubbed his nose into Carmel's cheek ruff. "If I'd trusted you…if I'd tried to contact you when I went to college, maybe…maybe we'd have talked. Maybe we could've stayed friends for some of the last fifteen years." Carmel started to talk, but Sierra cut him off. "Instead, I spent a few years being angry and not trusting anyone, and then a whole lot of time looking for you. I had a couple boyfriends I shared a bed and not much else with. Nobody ever touched me the way you did."

"Mmm." The coyote held him more tightly. "Before the morning, it was a pretty wonderful night there. I never got to tell you that."

"I don't just mean that," Sierra said, although the coyote's scent and the words were stirring memories of writhing bodies, of all the things he'd done that were even better because he was exploring them with Carmel. "I mean…"

"I know." Sierra could feel Carmel's grin in his words. "But it was pretty great. I still think about it a lot."

"Me too." Sierra relaxed his arms. Carmel did the same. They drew their muzzles back, until their noses were almost touching.

"I didn't win the game," Carmel said softly.

"What?"

"To get you away." The coyote's ears flattened. He lowered his muzzle, looking down at Sierra's chest. "I didn't win."

"But you got me away."

"Uh-huh." Carmel took a breath. "But that wasn't the point of the game." He lifted his muzzle and looked right at Sierra, and the snow leopard looked back, aware of his heartbeat, aware of the rising hope in him that maybe the fifteen years hadn't been completely wasted. So that he wouldn't embarrass himself, he pulled Carmel against him again and buried his nose in the coyote's shoulder.

"You can stay here tonight," Sierra said. "But I don't know if I want to…I mean, I did just see you with that jackrabbit, and, uh—"

Carmel lifted a paw. "Say no more. I can sleep on the floor."

"No, no." Sierra badly wanted those paws to stay around him. "I was going to say, I just had the pine marten in here, too."

The coyote canted his ears to the side. "How was he?"

The intimacy of the question took Sierra off guard. He laughed shortly and then rubbed his whiskers. "Squeaky. Nice guy, though. Look, I'll see how I feel in the morning. A good night's sleep…some chance to get used to this…"

"I'll see how I feel in the morning, too." Carmel smiled. "You're not the only one who doesn't feel up to doing anything tonight."

They sat like that for a moment longer, and then Sierra said, "Well. So. Crawl into bed with me?"

Carmel backed away, nodding, with a wide grin on his muzzle. He slid off the bed and stood up, his back to Sierra, shedding the bathrobe without hesitation.

A line of dark fur ran through the dusky tan, from the tuft between his ears to the tip of his tail. Slightly-muscled arms hung uncertainly at his sides, framing a slender build. His tail swished over his bare rear, and he looked over his shoulder. "Well," he said, "I figure you've already seen it all."

"Uh-huh." Sierra stayed where he was. "Turn around."

Carmel turned, slowly. The tan gave way to creamy ivory on his chest and stomach, and around the sheath and sac hanging between his legs. A little pink showed at the tip, extending farther out as Sierra watched, but Carmel made no move to hide it. He spread his arms. "Good?"

Sierra grinned and nodded. As Carmel lifted the covers and worked his way beneath them, Sierra hopped off the bed himself and walked around to his backpack. He shed his shirt and pants, and then turned off the light.

"No fair," Carmel said from the bed, though Sierra saw his eyes gleaming and was sure he could see perfectly well.

"Tough," Sierra said. "If you stay through the morning, you'll get another look."

Carmel was quiet, and Sierra briefly regretted the remark as he slid his boxers down his legs. He walked around the bed again, getting in on the side opposite Carmel. Again, the room was silent, but this time it was a silence of expectation.

"I can't believe I'm here in bed with you," Sierra said. "After all this time."

"I know." The coyote exhaled. "I wish we could just roll back the clock. Start over."

"We can tell ourselves that story." Sierra lay on his back, arms folded over his chest. "But it won't be real."

"It's as real as we make it."

"That's fine for other people." Sierra closed his eyes.

"You're telling yourself a story right now," Carmel said quietly. "You're telling yourself a story in which you've settled a score after fifteen years. You're trying to tell yourself that things are going to get better, that all the problems you've been having for the last fifteen years are gone."

"No," Sierra said. "My therapist told me not to expect that."

"Therapy is another story," Carmel said. His weight shifted, and Sierra caught his scent coming closer. A paw crept below the covers, brushing his side and then coming to rest on his stomach. "It's teaching you to tell yourself the story you need to hear to heal and go on."

The warmth on his stomach felt good. Sierra lay still, feeling the paw rise and fall with his breathing. "I don't know what story to tell myself.

But I don't think all my problems are going to disappear. I'm not that much of an idiot."

Carmel crept a little closer. "If I told you that story, would you listen?"

Sierra snorted. "I think it'll take a while before I'll believe one of your stories again."

"Mm." Carmel breathed across the pillow. A waft of mint came to Sierra. "Once upon a time," he said, "there were two guys who fell in love. Fifteen years later, they got another chance."

"It's not that easy."

"Of course not. Stories don't take on the first try. You have to tell them again and again to make them true."

Sierra didn't trust himself to say anything. But he moved his paw down and rested it atop Carmel's, and squeezed gently.

ABOUT THE AUTHOR

Kyell Gold began writing furry fiction a long, long time ago. In the early days of the 21st century, he got up the courage to write some gay furry romance, first publishing his story "The Prisoner's Release" in Sofawolf Press's adult magazine **Heat**. He has since won twelve Ursa Major awards for his stories and novels, and his acclaimed novel *Out of Position* co-won the Rainbow Award for Best Gay Novel of 2009. His novel "Green Fairy" was nominated for inclusion in the ALA's "Over the Rainbow" list for 2012.

He was not born in California, but now considers it his home. He loves to travel and dine out with his partner of many years, Kit Silver, and can be seen at furry conventions in California, around the country, and abroad. More information about him and his books is available at *http://www.kyellgold.com.*

ABOUT THE ARTIST

Sabretoothed Ermine is a Canadian artist who has been doing "furry" art full-time since 2009 and, despite what people may say about turning a hobby into a career, still loves it. Though she hasn't attended any art schools (that would mean moving to a city, ugh!) she has been drawing since she could hold a pencil, and anthropomorphic animals have always been her subject of choice. You may see her at a convention now and again, but like most weasels she's generally pretty reclusive and happy to stay with her husband in their beautiful forested homeland of British Columbia.

All of her furry art and her current commission info can be found in her FurAffinity gallery at: *www.furaffinity.net/user/sabretoothedermine/*

Or if you just want to say hi, feel free to email her at: *ermine@ ermineart.com*

ABOUT CUPCAKES

Cupcakes are novellas, with more substance than short stories, though not as long as novels. The Cupcakes line was developed for FurPlanet by foozzzball, Kyell Gold, and Rikoshi as a reaction to their desire to tell novella-length stories and the lack of publishing opportunities for novellas.

Previous Cupcakes have been nominated twice for Ursa Major awards, winning once. "Winter Games" is the fifth in the line produced by those three authors.

ABOUT THE PUBLISHER

FurPlanet publishes original works of furry fiction. You can explore their selection at *http://www.furplanet.com.*